SAINT BOB DAY

K. C. WILSON

Black Rose Writing | Texas

ISBN: 978-1-68433-307-3
PUBLISHED BY BLACK ROSE WRITING
www.blackrosewriting.com

Printed in the United States of America
Suggested Retail Price (SRP) $17.95

Saint Bob Day is printed in Plantagenet Cherokee

For Robert Hayes

SAINT BOB DAY

CHAPTER ONE
WELCOME TO THE LODGE AND CLUB

In the maintenance department of the Belle Rive Lodge and Club, the secret sport of nicknaming leavened the sameness of days with the lifeblood of sanity.

A gifted nicknamer, Bob Day, also the lead technician, carried a step ladder through the Innlet Lounge area on the mezzanine at teatime. Fit, though slight of frame and bald at sixty-one, he positioned the ladder under a bad bulb between tables reserved for members and guests.

Each weekday afternoon from three to four, the Lodge served High Tea in the Innlet Lounge. Petit four sandwiches, cookies and pastries attracted a regular clientele of society matrons and doyennes. For a core group of members, it was an integral part of their day. None were more devoted to High Tea than Mama Muumuu.

Her garment of choice was a blue paisley housedress that looked very comfortable and might have been appropriate, with its matching slippers, in almost any venue once. Yet every day she wore, if not the same muumuu, another just like it, of a slightly different hue. She wore the muumuu like a uniform. It had earned her the undisputed nickname.

From the third step, Bob glanced down over the balustrade at the lobby below and noted the onset of shift change at the reception desk where Naila and Constance stood side by side bickering in undertones.

To Bob, Naila was Queen Noor. Constance was She Who Shall Not Be Named. None of Bob's nicknames had ever stuck to Constance. Someone else had named her That Bitch.

Beyond the Paraguayan mahogany doors, the head bellman, Don, nicknamed with minimum effort, Just Don, waited under the porte-cochere for a black Lincoln bearing the celebrated Senator from Alabama. He uttered, "Any day now," into the microphone attached to his collar.

At the reception desk, Naila, a dynamic internationalist, was transitioning with her evening shift manager, Constance Featherton, of the Wimauma Feathertons, whom Naila loathed for thousands of reasons.

Constance, a fortyish platinum blonde, noted a bulge in Naila's handbag the size of a wine bottle. A faint whistle in her exhalation thinly veiled oenophilic hauteur.

Naila ignored her. "Copy, Don," she spoke into her microphone.

"You may leave," said Constance. "You wouldn't want to be late for whatever party you might be late for. I'll see to Senator Rutland."

Constance's fingertip grazed the shell of her blonde facade, and a professional hotelier's smile appeared to animate the vacancy of her cartoonish facial features. Poised behind the granite desk, she stood ready for the next opportunity to embody the hotel's five-diamond standard of hospitality.

Beside her, Naila lingered at her own terminal. She said, "I wouldn't dream of leaving yet. Senator Rutland's a dear friend, one of my all-time favorite guests."

"Please don't feel you have to stay," said Constance.

Naila said, "Just a bit longer. To say hello. Although my husband will be wanting his dinner. He's always hungry after performing surgery. That is so strange. I could not eat."

"But if you must, go," said Constance.

Constance happened to look up and made eye contact with Bob. What she took as a tight smile was actually Bob wincing over the chafe of damp underwear. His socks also still felt wet inside his shoes.

"Bob's creeping me out," Constance said to Naila. "He's stalking me."

"Bob is not stalking you," said Naila. "He's changing a light bulb."

Constance muttered Bob's name like a curse. "Him and his nicknames."

"You have terrible taste in men," said Naila. "Everyone knows that. Bob is a very fine man."

Bob was wearing the spare uniform he had kept in his locker, socks and underwear not included.

Earlier that afternoon, Bob had entered the "wet area" of the men's locker room on a mission to replace a defective shower head. Two naked members sat on teak benches by the Jacuzzi reading The *Wall Street*

Journal while a third, their elder, a deeply tanned octogenarian, stood waist deep in the bubbling hot water.

The gym staff all knew the Slow Walker by his given name, Ben Bancroft, but with no disrespect intended, he was far more widely identified as the Slow Walker. He always took very small steps, yet never relied on a walker or a cane.

After his daily laps, it was Mr. Bancroft's habit to complete his ritual with ten minutes in the Jacuzzi followed by a cool shower. The water temperature in the Jacuzzi was kept as a rule at one hundred and eight degrees Fahrenheit; warm, by any standard, and actually rather hot. Posted warnings recommended no more than fifteen-minute sessions. Perhaps he lingered a bit longer in the hot water that day while Bob replaced the shower head.

When Bob came out of the shower to find the Slow Walker floating face down in the churning bubbles, he kicked his shoes off and jumped in. The two *Wall Street Journal* readers, once roused, helped Bob drag Ben Bancroft out of the water. The three of them rolled his inert body onto the tiles, and Bob administered CPR.

Someone on the gym staff called 911. But Bob got the Slow Walker breathing again. By the time the EMTs arrived, Ben Bancroft was drinking coffee.

Bob's boss, Ed Nogg, the Head of the Maintenance Department, told Bob to take the rest of the day off, but Bob had insisted on finishing his shift.

As he stepped down from his ladder, Bob heard Mama Muumuu gag and hiccup. He saw that a crusty corner was bitten off of the cranberry scone on her plate. Her airway was blocked, her face a deep red.

The two other ladies at her table gasped in horror. One cried, "Help!"

Mama Muumuu slumped forward, her head almost to the table. Bob situated himself behind her and inserted his hands like blades under her armpits and then pushed his arms in up to his elbows and pressed the heel of his palm under her breasts against her diaphragm.

"When I lift her, pull the chair away," he commanded the matron to her left.

Bob heaved her up, and the chair came up with her. The helpful woman separated the chair from Mama Muumuu's behind, and Bob leaned back with her weight against his chest. He bounced once and came down hard on his heels as he gave her a high, tight squeeze. Out came a spit chunk of pastry crust. The hard kernel landed like a bullet on her plate. Her airway opened with a wheeze.

Bob released her. She looked up at his face with wonder.

"You touched my breast," she said.

"I apologize," said Bob.

"The Heimlich maneuver," said the woman who helped. "We're so glad you were here."

"Yes, thank you," said Mama Muumuu. "I think you may have saved my life."

"You wonderful, wonderful man," said the other woman at the table.

Bob looked around the Innlet Lounge area. All eyes were on him.

Pete, the bartender, said, 'Let's hear it for Bob!"

As one, the High Tea attendees began clapping for Bob.

He gravitated toward the bar as the soft applause faded. He said to Pete. "I could use a drink."

Pete said, "Everyone's watching. I would, but you know."

"Of course," said Bob.

Apart from the High Tea set, a young couple with a toddler sat at the table nearest the piano. The black Steinway was situated in an alcove near the restrooms a couple of feet from the stone balustrade overlooking the lobby below. The man kept his leering eyes on the piano. The mother had her hands full with the little boy, who kept climbing and jumping from chair to chair.

The man slid onto the piano bench and uncovered the keys.

"Don't," the mother warned.

"I have to," he said.

He looked around the room and saw that no one was watching. He closed his eyes and began a soft glissando.

The piano was not strictly off limits. From time to time guests or members felt the urge to tickle the ivories and no one ever objected except the entertainer who played on weekends, for whom the piano was kept in tune. Most of the time, the dabblers did no harm.

The regular member crowd was older, established, and traditionally conservative. Some of them may have been hell raisers once, but that was long ago.

The father's playing was reminiscent of bygone romance,

sentimental and seductive.

"They should hire that guy," said Bob. "He's better than the woman who plays on weekends."

Pete agreed. "He's not bad."

Bob looked at his watch. "Well, time to go schmooze with the queen."

"Swing back by," said Pete. "I'll have one for you to go."

"Tempting, but no," said Bob.

Bob carried his ladder past the piano and returned it to its spot in the storage closet inside the men's restroom. As he returned to the common area and moved past the piano again to take the stairs down to the lobby, the mother placed the tyke on top of the piano and headed into the ladies restroom.

The father began toying with the opening chords of *Piano Man*.

Bob descended the stairs into the lobby. The father began to sing, his voice in immediate, dire conflict with his technical prowess.

"Oh, ladidah-dididah-ah, laladididah-ah-ah ..."

Alone behind the reception desk, Naila was busy with a guest and had no time to schmooze with Bob. Constance had retreated into her private office.

Bob took a step back from the front area. He was just going to wave, but Naila did not look up.

The table climbing toddler, less than spellbound by his father's performance, continued to squirm around on the piano. In the shuddering blink of an eye, he managed to bridge the two-foot distance from the piano to the flat top of the balustrade and was sitting on it with his back to the lobby when his mother emerged from the restroom. She saw the boy on the balustrade and shrieked.

The father opened his eyes, startled out of his reverie, and lunged for the boy who leaned back out of his reach and fell twenty feet toward the travertine marble floor of the lobby.

The boy would have landed hard had Bob not taken a second step back in reflex to the mother's shriek and looked up in time to see her child falling safely into his arms.

The boy, caught like a Hail Mary pass, began to wail. The mother and father leaned over the balustrade and saw their child in Bob's arms. Both of their faces with jaws dropped and eyes rounded in surprise and shock imprinted themselves in the fabric of Bob's memory in one eternal second.

The parents rushed down the stairs. The mother hugged Bob with gratitude so fierce it felt she might never release him. Then she turned furious eyes on the father, who could not endure the reproach in them and took her place, hugging Bob almost as fiercely.

"Thank you, my friend," he whispered. "Oh, my God, thank you, sir."

"Is there anything else I can do for you today?" Bob said.

The father did not seem to recognize that oft-repeated motto as a witticism.

"I hope not," he said.

Everyone in the lounge upstairs was drawn to the balustrade railing to watch as everyone in the lobby below stood by in silence at the moment of the child's reunion with his parents. A cry went up, and the people were all in unison saying "Bob, Bob, Bob!"

Naila came out from behind the front desk to give Bob a huge hug.

In the surreal moment, Bob saw the long black Lincoln Town Car approach the entrance to the Lodge and park under the porte-cochere. Some nascent part of his consciousness recognized the car and understood what the Senator's return would mean to him, personally, but for a brief time he kept floating on clouds of cotton, supported by angels. Safe in their arms. Like a baby.

Constance reappeared behind the front desk, perplexed at all the commotion. She saw everyone fawning over her arch nemesis, Bob.

With an uncertain smile, she asked Naila, "What's all this?"

"Bob caught a baby," said Naila.

"He what?" Constance asked.

"That baby fell off the balcony," said Naila. "Bob caught him."

The lobby grew quiet around Constance, as if to measure her response. She mustered all the enthusiasm she could and said, "Wow, Bob. Wow."

Attention passed from her back to the parents and the baby. Bob edged away from the melee. It was time to go. His day was done.

Behind the desk, Constance composed herself.

Naila heard her mutter under her breath, "Bob caught a baby! Whoop de do."

It was a day without equal in the annals of the Lodge. As Bob walked through the halls and passed outside through the loading dock gates, he felt like clouds were all around him. Walls of cotton enfolded him, raised him up and supported him as if he were being carried.

Just Don stood by the Lincoln while the Senator completed a phone call. At a nod, he opened the Senator's door. "Welcome back to the Lodge, Senator Rutland. Great to have you with us again."

The doughy gentleman behind the wheel looked none the worse for having driven several hundred miles. His socks and tie hung from the pockets of his seersucker slacks. Barefoot in Bass Weejuns, a salmon Gant shirt and aviator shades, the senator brushed Cheese Nip crumbs from his lap as he stepped out.

"Great to be back in Florida, Don."

He accepted a valet receipt for his keys and passed Don a generous tip in a hearty handclasp, dismissing his token protest before it was uttered.

A second bellman opened the carved mahogany door and held it for him.

The Senator read the gold plated name tag on the bellman's black vest. "Thank you, Mikhail," he said. "You from Alabama?"

"No, sir. Bosnia," said Mikhail.

"Ah," said the Senator. "Dobar."

Behind the reception desk, Constance beamed conviviality. "Why, Senator Rutland," she gushed, "what a treat to have you back with us again here at the Lodge and Club."

"I do love this place," he said. "Y'all always make me feel so welcome."

Across the lobby to the east, through the double doors and the window wall, the Atlantic Ocean glowed in a soft pinkish light. Small waves rolled in, lapping against the shins of a man in a straw hat, fishing in the shallows. A few blue umbrellas and chairs remained on the beach.

The Senator watched the fisherman and the ocean and the hazy tinted sky while he listened with one ear to Constance's mildly flirtatious patter. She also was from the south, although South Florida hardly qualified as the south in the Senator's judgment. She might as well have been from South New Jersey. The Senator didn't know why he bothered anymore, but there was something about Constance that made him want to ruffle her feathers.

"Wimauma, that's down near Tampa, isn't it? Down there where the carnie folk live. Connie, are your people carnies?"

Constance raised her nose a fraction. "Only the Gibtown Feathertons," she said.

The Senator snapped his fingers, as if an old memory had just fallen into place. "I met a Raleigh Featherington down there once around Gibsontown, a poker player, very unscrupulous."

"Everybody knows Uncle Raleigh," said Constance.

"That old carnie skinned me alive. Taught me a lesson I'll never forget."

Constance looked up with a cocked eyebrow. "Don't play poker with carnies?"

"You got that right," said the Senator. "But you know, some of us never learn."

Constance slid an amenities folder and a digital room key card across the granite counter.

"Is there anything else I can do for you today?" she asked.

"Probably not," said the Senator. "But if you think of something, call me."

Mikhail stood by to escort the Senator to his room.

In the parking garage, Don loaded the Senator's luggage onto a brass valet trolley and left it by the north elevator while he parked the Town Car in a nearby slot. He returned and wheeled the trolley into the north elevator. He punched the button, and the elevator doors had just begun to close as two middle-aged maintenance men, one bald and uniformed in shades of blue, the other balding, wearing paint-splattered whites, passed by the elevator doors in a golf cart.

At the end of their shift that day, a Thursday, Bob the Nicknamer and Karl the Painter were on their way to the housekeeping office, home of the digital time clock, at the opposite end of the parking garage. The two senior members of the maintenance staff acknowledged Don with soft salutes as the elevator doors closed on him and the Senator's load.

Seconds later, the golf cart was halfway to the south elevator when Naila called out Bob's name. Karl tapped the brake and turned the cart around. Although neither a manager nor a supervisor, Naila and no other wore the imaginary crown in the reception area.

She had developed a congenial rapport with Bob.

In the beginning it was hardly so. Naila's imperious tone had incensed Bob. He had found her regal mannerisms pretentious. And she was slow to appreciate his wit.

"I'm very busy right now. I'll have to call you back," she would say and hang up when Bob would call the front desk to inquire after the status of a room, whether it was vacant, occupied or up for arrival. Too frequently, she would neglect to call him back.

Bob's original nickname for Naila was "the Untouchable," but at some point, their chemistry had ceased to clash. Bob had worn her down with puns and quips and clever wordplay. Now she would smile when she saw Bob coming, ready with quips of her own to match his. Now they were bantering buddies, exchanging endearing ripostes. With a radical change of heart, he had renamed her Queen Noor.

In one of her many pale mint suits she stood waiting for the golf cart to slow to a stop by her car so she could talk to Bob. She held a crumpled brown bag with a bottle in it, the paper twisted around the neck.

"Bob," she began, "Mister Bob, we are so fortunate, are we not, to work in such a place with such fine individuals, on whom we can depend and to whom we can turn and rely upon to help us out in situations that might seem awkward or worse, otherwise. Do you know what I mean?"

Bob looked at her, neither nodding nor smiling. His attentiveness suggested amusement, but that would have been an assumption. "This woman," she continued, "a guest, Bob, she gave me this bottle of wine as a gift. And I, well, I don't even drink much, hardly at all, anymore, Bob, I don't, no matter what people say about me." Her pause was briefer than a wink, a self-deprecatory chuckle. "And I would not have hurt this woman's feelings for the world, so I took this gift of hers, thinking of the many wonderful people working here at the Lodge with us who might appreciate it. Not that you came immediately to mind, Bob, but there you were, and after today, my God, you are my hero, and so, why not Bob? I thought, maybe, at the very least, you know some deserving soul who would appreciate this not particularly good wine, but maybe it's not so bad. Or maybe, who knows, Bob? May I just give this to you?"

Bob let her place the brown bag in his hands. "Well, I never," he said.

"Thank you, Bob," said the Queen. "Thank you so much."

As she climbed into her Lexus, Karl eased the cart forward, pulled a wide U-turn and headed back toward the Housekeeping Office to punch out for the day. Bob granted the bottle in the brown bag no more scrutiny than a single disinterested glance at its screw top.

"I can't drink this swill," he said.

Karl reached over and slid the top of the bag down the neck of the bottle, revealing the label. "Strawberry Blush" White Zinfandel. "Oh boy, wine," Karl grinned.

Bob looked at him sideways.

"Bob," said Karl, "you can live a hundred years. It won't get any better than this. Today was the very best day of your life. It's all downhill from here."

CHAPTER TWO
UNDERCOVER

In Bob's first Employee of the Month commendation, Head of Maintenance, Edwin Nogg, had described him as "unfailingly polite." While that description was more accurate and less burdensome to Bob during his first year on the job than in his second, his stellar conduct had gained the endorsement, with rare exceptions, of the rank and file of his fellow employees. He had but one abiding enemy at the Lodge, the bane of his existence, Constance Featherton, of the Wimauma Feathertons.

Constance and Bob interacted daily and were often barely civil to each other on the phone. As was the case with Naila in the beginning, it seemed likely that their mutual antipathy masked repressed attractions on both sides, but no, Bob had assured Karl when the painter first floated that wrong idea past him like a conversational trial balloon. No, Bob insisted, in no uncertain terms. There was no love lost between them.

Bob's ready wit drew on a treasury of pithy quotes and truisms. But his attempts to enliven mundane communications with Constance were met with condescension, blank stares and supercilious sighs. Her failure to recognize in Bob the Bodhisattva of poise had led to her fateful error of attempting to browbeat him.

Karl said, "So, She Who Shall Not Be Named has seen your dark side."

"Only an inkling," said Bob.

The two maintenance men were overlooking the ocean side pool area where bathing beauties of all ages basked in the morning sun.

"NQ rising," said Karl.

The "Nubility Quotient," baseline indicator of nubile pulchritude, could rise as high as eleven or drop to flat zero, depending on the median age and beauty of the clientele. Karl, not Bob, had introduced the cryptic term into their lexicon. If anyone had a dark side, it was Karl, not Bob. Between them, the term, "NQ," was impenetrable code.

Bob wore rimless progressive lens bifocals, photo gradient, designed to darken in the sun, a smooth union of function and style. Of average height, he did not smoke. At work, he walked more than he ever rode or drove the golf cart and took the stairs instead of elevators unless burdened by tools.

Karl, in contrast, hated walking and always took the golf cart, and the elevator.

"Look at you," Karl teased, "eyeing little girls with bad intent. Dark Bob, that's who you really are."

Bob cracked a glacial smirk.

"You should have a website called bobsdarkside.com," said Karl, "where you can freely explore your alter ego, Dark Bob."

Four years earlier, Bob had come to the Lodge as a new hire with no previous experience in the hotel industry or in any field of maintenance. An avid watcher of *This Old House* and eminently teachable, he had learned at the foot of the retired master chief, Ed Nogg, how to handle most recurring plumbing and electrical problems. He'd met the challenges of steep learning curves in all areas of hotel maintenance except painting, for which he retained a stubborn lack of interest, and in record time had set a benchmark standard of competence.

Karl, slightly younger than Bob, had five years under his belt at the Lodge.

"Do you have one of those sites?" Bob asked.

"I don't need one," said Karl. "This job is my alter ego. I'm undercover forty hours a week, living the dream of another day in paradise. And, Bob, if you ever quit or get fired, I'll have no one at all to talk to. You're my link to sanity in this place. If they ever get an inkling of the extent of my dubiety, I'll be fired instantly."

Bob was watching Claudia, the Columbian jogger, recede into the misty distance down the shoreline. A "Claudia sighting" would soften Bob's demeanor with wistful reverence.

"See how she prances," Bob said, as if uttering a prayer. Karl was near enough to hear the private, winsome gasp of involuntary longing.

Bob and Karl appeared to be examining the railing for discrepancies as they moved down the seawall to a closer vantage point from which to watch Claudia turn and head back toward them.

Each day brought a fresh promise of another Claudia sighting.

"Look at us," said Karl, "shadows of our former selves, lurking like voyeurs. Furtive, pathetic, invisible to the objects of our delight, and resigned, for the most part, to invisibility, except in the case of Claudia, who, at forty-something, still stokes our undead embers with a more exquisite body than any woman half her age."

Claudia in her black knit shorts, her perfect legs pumping in graceful rhythm grew near. They both dropped their eyes as she passed by and lifted them in time to watch her single black braid swish and sway across the middle of her back.

"Did you see the way she looked at me?" said Karl.

"I did not," said Bob.

"Bob, I think she might be too much for me."

Bob watched Claudia until she disappeared.

"Seriously, Bob," said Karl. "I need this job. My kid needs insurance. Please don't ever quit or get fired."

"I've no plan to go anywhere, anytime soon," said Bob.

That was the day before yesterday, when days at the Lodge were still more or less typical.

CHAPTER THREE
PROTOCOLS OF THE NAKED ELDERS

A typical day for Bob included frequent encounters with one or more naked men. In the men's locker room of the Belle Rive Lodge and Club, the nonsensical credo, "Another Day in Paradise," offered broad irony to counter the sight of a hoary ancient blow drying his groin with a hair dryer, one foot planted on the marble sink, insensate scrotum flapping like a wet towel in the hot breeze, or of the conclaves of naked financial geniuses seated behind newspapers around the Jacuzzi, or of a butt scrubber flossing his nether ravine with a towel.

Such humdrum spectacles anaesthetized the uniformed staff to various degrees, from the nonplussed Filipino housemen, Edelberto and Rey, who conversed in Tagalog saying God knew what as they supplied Lodge members and guests with an infinity of clean yellow towels, to the crew of maintenance men who responded with jaundiced eyes lowered to various random calls of distress from the Fitness Center.

Two doors opened from the locker room to the wet area. Against one wall a table laden with clean towels and a used towel bin took up too much room near one of the doors. The General Manager of the Lodge, David Moriarty, once suggested to Ed Nogg, that a customized piece of furniture might be designed, built and finished like a cabinet, as a possible alternative to the towel table, to enhance the display and disposal of clean and used towels, thereby also alleviating congestion in the narrow aisle caused by the door opening onto the existing towel table.

David's suggestion was duly noted by Ed Nogg, whose inner zealotry would not allow him to refuse a challenge.

What David requested, David would get. A custom built towel drop cabinet was not in any sense expected to pose a problem.

Ed Nogg happened to mention the upcoming project to a working carpenter, Roger, who had contracted and performed other work for the

Lodge. Roger took measurements and discussed design with Ed and, in advance of final authorization, he built the cabinet with poplar plywood, in accordance with Ed's original specs, and expected to be paid six hundred dollars for it.

Ed said, "Roger, I asked you for an estimate. I didn't ask you to build it yet."

"Well, there it is," said Roger.

Surprised by the sudden appearance of the towel cabinet, Ed Nogg knew very well that David, also known as King David, Davidicus Maximus, and even, to some, the Princess, was unlikely to authorize six hundred dollars for its construction. It was supposedly still a tentative project, one of countless capital improvement issues. Yet there it was, already built. And before it could be put in place, it would have to be painted and made presentable. But to paint it indicated acceptance, and then he would have no recourse but to pay for it.

Not accepting it would have been the thing to do, but Ed Nogg did not do that, because he had his painter there poised with a bucket of primer and a brush in hand. He trusted Karl to pretty it up.

Ed paid Roger with his own money, against his better judgment, and Karl painted the cabinet, inside and out, with two coats of oil enamel. Many people looked at the cabinet as the gleaming paint dried and remarked upon its inelegance, but all agreed it was well painted.

The question was, would David Moriarty approve the bill and reimburse Ed Nogg?

When the day came for the towel drop cabinet to be installed, it was loaded onto the back of the golf cart and moved from the workspace outside the maintenance shop across the street to the fitness center, where it was placed on a furniture mover and pushed through three doorways to its designated spot against the wall by the door leading out to the wet area. There were by then a few naysayers who predicted it would be too large for the space. Bob and Karl fit the ungainly cabinet into the slotted area where it was screwed into the wall with four long bolts.

Bob squatted next to the cabinet, drill motor in one hand, bolts in the other, eye level with the genitalia of a fat old man who squeezed by Bob on his way to the wet area saying, "'S'cuse me." Seconds later, the old man returned to retrieve something from his locker, and squeezed past

Bob again with the same, "'S'cuse me."

Committed to his task, Bob did not get up or move or stop or acknowledge the man in any way, except to say, "Sir, we'll be out of your way directly."

Soon the man was back again, saying "'S'cuse me," as he snaked past Bob once more, his naked groin inches from Bob's right ear, or had he but turned his head, Bob's face.

No one laughed about it until they got back to the shop. Bob didn't laugh at all about it, even then.

Within twenty-four hours, the word came down from on high that the members hated the towel drop cabinet. David hated it, too. He hated it so much that he disputed the six hundred dollar bill and refused to reimburse Ed Nogg. He claimed he had never authorized its construction and was furious to learn that the bill had already been paid. David insisted that he had merely asked for an estimate. Ed Nogg agreed that that was certainly the case, and volunteered to cancel his request for reimbursement.

Relations soured instantly between the Lodge and Roger. He would receive no more work contracts. The towel drop was removed and replaced with a smaller towel table. The monstrosity was then placed in the storage area outside the maintenance shop, covered with a large dropcloth and forgotten as much as possible.

What was not forgotten, what would never be forgotten, was the look on Bob's face as that fat old man kept squeezing past him, balls out at Bob's eye level, saying "'S'cuse me, 's'cuse me, 's'cuse me."

CHAPTER FOUR
COWBOY UP

Bob had a lot on his mind as he drove home that day. Things had changed since morning. Karl thought his life at the Lodge was undercover. He had no idea what being undercover meant. No one did.

The liquor store up ahead looked like the end of the rainbow. Then he remembered the magnum in his freezer, a birthday gift from Ed Nogg and the boys. Half-full or half-empty, either way. Choosing to be a half-full kind of guy paid no concrete benefits, but neither did pessimism.

He steered his black truck off the road into the Ocean Oaks apartment complex, slowing to ease over speed bumps and parked in front of his one bedroom unit. "And here we are," he said out loud to the old guy in the rearview mirror, "you and me."

He cut the motor and sat for a moment while the engine ticked and cooled. He gathered his things, his wet uniform and his cell phone and carried them inside.

There was no mail, nor any phone messages.

Bob opened the freezer and pulled out the vodka. He poured a double shot into a clean glass, took a taste and carried it with the bottle over to a small desk. He booted up his computer and took another taste. He checked his email, nothing important. He clicked on **New** and typed an email:

First of all, I don't want to move. I don't want to be moved. I have no intention of moving. And finally, I'm not moving. However, we may have a problem.

He typed in an email address and sat back in his chair and looked at the message. The glass in his hand was empty. He poured another double shot and hit *Send.*

Bob did not look around the room. There was nothing to look at, no pictures on the walls. The room was bare and beige, and he liked it that way. He knew where everything was in the dark. Chair, table, couch, bed, TV, dresser, closet, kitchenette, computer. There were no toys to trip over, no clutter, no pets. Bob took off his shoes and the phone rang.

He answered on the second ring, "Hello."

"You don't have to be such a little girl about it." The voice on the phone belonged to Berne Ventine, of the U.S. Marshals Service.

Aside from his daughter and Berne Ventine, no one was supposed to know that Bob was in the WitSec Program. In his former life as Bob Deighton, he had testified in the trial of Larry "the Cherry" Wilhoite, formerly Aronoyad Wilgushku, whose business enterprises were allied with associates of the so-called "Dixie Mafia" and included the "Cherry Red" employment agency, which specialized in supplying VIPs with English speaking au pairs and nannies from Russia as well as discreet "Russian Brides" and sex workers to offshore oil rig workers in the Gulf of Mexico. Also, he had masterminded the interstate transport of electronic bingo machines across state lines, a felonious act for which he was convicted under the State of Alabama's anti-gambling regulations.

Bob Deighton, an executive with a well-known trucking company, had come forward in support of the state's anti-corruption drive, but his decision to testify against Wilhoite had led to his termination sans severance package.

Threats and warnings delivered to him through intermediaries promised repercussions to himself and to his daughter. Bob contacted the U.S. Marshals Service and requested assistance. He and his daughter, Eliza, were given new identities and relocated to Florida.

Bob Deighton became Bob Day. No big stretch.

Eliza had married a soldier and moved to another state. Their son, Timmy, was two-and-a-half, almost three now. Bob had not seen his grandson in eleven months. Originally, the plan was for him to live near his daughter so that they would be able to help each other adjust to their new identities. Eliza had kept in touch, but it seemed to Bob that they were not nearly as close as they had been a few years earlier.

"The Senator's back," said Bob.

"Yeah, I meant to tell you," said Berne Ventine.

"You meant to tell me? What else did you mean to tell me?"

"Easy, big fella, where's your sense of humor?"

"Right now it's just south of my taint," said Bob, "which is chafed raw from being left out of the loop."

"Come on. You see the hotel reservations. You knew he was coming back."

"I didn't hear it from you, though, did I?"

"Did he see you?"

"No. Last time, he didn't even recognize me."

"You can't be certain of that."

"I dropped fifty pounds since the trial."

"It's all good, then," said Berne. "Now all you have to do is get back to that low profile."

"Berne, I don't want to end up on the news," said Bob.

"Your antics today suggest otherwise," said Berne. "Nice work, by the way. For the record, I'm speechless."

"I'm not starting over," said Bob.

"I get it. You're settled in. You love your life."

"If I have to make a stand, this is as good a place as any."

"Bob, I'm hearing cowboy talk. I don't condone it. Outlaw Josey Wales talk. I won't support it."

"Wilhoite's out, isn't he? You should have told me. Is he out?"

"Get some rest, Bob. I'll make some calls."

"He's getting out early. Son of a bitch. And you didn't tell me."

"Lest you forget, Bob," said Berne Ventine, "I knew Josey Wales. Josey Wales was a friend of mine. Believe me, you're no Josey Wales."

"I want an update tomorrow," said Bob. "And don't ever use that line on me again."

Bob replaced the receiver. He drained the glass and went in to take a shower.

Later that evening, Bob cleaned his gun of choice, the Sig Arms GSR 1911 45 ACP. The automatic cartridge pistol held eight rounds in the magazine. He racked the slide ejecting the bullet in the chamber, ejected the magazine and popped it back in. He pulled the slide back and the cartridge reloaded. He set the safety and replaced the weapon in a desk drawer.

Bob felt like he should call his daughter, but she was in a different time zone. He was tired, and a little bit slammed after that last drink and not sure what he would even want to tell her, except that he loved her and she knew that. It would have alarmed her if that were all he had called to say.

Better to wait and see what tomorrow had in store.

CHAPTER FIVE
PRICE OF FAME

Sunrise brought its worshippers and their dogs. An array of regulars found mornings at the Lodge the perfect time and place to begin the hours of leisure that would link together and comprise their day. Retirees who lived nearby were either members themselves or accompanied members whose membership key cards opened the South Gate, allowing access to the property and the beach. Fitness buffs, beachcombers, yoga and "Doga" classes, (yoga with and for dogs) coffee drinkers, newspaper and book readers; they came each morning to watch the sacred sunrise over the ocean.

That moment of morning grace belonged to them, and the brokedown majesty of the Lodge was theirs, as well. For members, the Oasis poolside oceanfront bar/restaurant was a second home. The Mediterranean style architecture of the Lodge, with its arches and columns and weathered pale stucco walls, terra cotta roof tiles and palm trees rooted in coquina imbued the landscape with old world flavor, but with the constant onslaught of sun and salt, the Lodge's aura of faded elegance required constant cosmetic attention.

The long hotel sprawled for two full blocks, nestled behind a sand dune where wild rabbits hid among the brambles and foraged through hardy welters of weeds, sea oats and blooming cactus flowers. Sixty-six guest rooms faced the ocean, each with its own sunrise view.

The poolside deck with its adjacent outside bar and restaurant was vacant and still during those dawn hours. The Oasis served lunch and dinner, no breakfast. Early risers found serenity at the sunny tables. Beauty surrounded the Lodge each morning.

From the western side of the building, always in shade before noon, Bob approached and took in the view. At seven a.m. the landscape lights still illuminated the bushes, and the sconce lights in the corridors still glowed. Set to a timer, sometimes the lights all turned off at the very moment Bob crossed the threshold into the garage, almost as if in response to his arrival, almost as if to say, "Welcome Home, Mr. Day."

Bob always came in around seven but would not punch in until seven-thirty. He'd open the shop, unplug the battery charger from the golf cart and back the cart out of the shop. He'd make a pot of his famous java, a stern blend with very little water. While it perked, he'd play phone messages and scan emails that had collected overnight. Each day there were one or more from King David, requesting updates on the status of projects. The tone of his emails reflected the moods of the Princess King and set the governing tone of the day.

Ed Nogg had granted Bob password access to his computer as a gesture of ultimate trust and respect. Since Bob had become a "supervisor," Ed's fondness for Bob had risen into the stratosphere. In the maintenance shop, you were either Bob or you were not Bob. If you were not Bob, the occasional shadow of Ed's disfavor fell upon you. It did not fall upon Bob.

Bob was the golden paragon, even before his day of days. It was a testament to his character that no one in the maintenance shop begrudged his favored status. No one aspired to compete for Ed's esteem. Bob filled a void, and the void was filled. He was the key that unlocked Ed Nogg. In Bob, Ed had found a buddy and a friend, a better buddy and a better friend than Karl or any other Lodge maintenance employee could ever be. Only Bob possessed the ideal temperament that enabled Ed to shine forth in his best light. Ed Nogg would have been bereft without him. He was tolerant yet unimpressed with anyone who was not Bob.

At seven-thirty, Bob had a Styrofoam cup in his hand. He stood in his usual spot near the door with his left foot propped on the portable air compressor as Karl arrived.

"Morning, Bob," said Karl.

"Morning, Karl."

Karl headed for the coffee pot. "What fresh hell faces us today?"

The phone rang. "Here we go," said Bob, picking up the phone.

"Good morning, maintenance. This is Bob."

The Queen said, "Good morning, Bob. "And how are you this fine day after?"

"Fine, and you?"

"Wonderful. Bob, I have someone here who wants to meet you."

"And who might that be?" Bob asked.

"A reporter from the local paper is here to interview you."

"Oh, no," said Bob. "No. No, I don't find that a sound idea."

"Oh, yes," said Naila. "Bob, you can't go around saving people's lives and expect no one to notice. It doesn't work that way in America."

"The land of the free? I am free to not participate in my own demise, am I not?"

"Oh, Bob, don't be a scaredy-cat," said Naila. "How does that song end, Bob, is it the home of the shy? No. It's the home of the brave, Bob. That's you. The brave. Come on. We're all so proud of you."

"I prefer not to."

Naila lowered her voice. "Bob, trust me. Just meet her."

"Her?" said Bob.

"Oh, did I fail to mention? Sorry. Yes, Bob. Trust me. I am your friend."

"I'll be there in a minute," said Bob.

"What's up?" said Karl.

"Nothing."

"You would prefer not to what?"

"Be interviewed," said Bob.

"Oh, pshaw," said Karl. "Hey, make sure they spell my name right."

Bob took the golf cart and headed for the bell stand.

At the front door chatting with Just Don and two other bellmen stood Shania Doyle. She was the redhead with the notebook and the camera. At twenty-five, fresh out of graduate school at UF, she was destined for bigger and better things than a human interest puff piece for the Lifestyles section, but her bright hazel eyes seized Bob's attention as he drove up in the cart and she would not let him go until she got her story.

Her smile did him in. She was younger than his daughter, and he found himself in short order grinning back at her, almost uncontrollably. She left Don and the other two bellmen at the bell stand and stepped across the cobblestones under the porte-cochere with her hand extended.

"Mr. Robert Day? So pleased to meet you. I'm Shania Doyle from The Times-Union."

"Charmed," said Bob. He sat frozen behind the wheel of the cart, struggling to control the rush of youthful impulses. The bellmen mugged behind her back, puckering up silent smooches.

"Would you like to take a ride," Bob asked.

"I'd love to," she said and joined him on the cart. Bob pulled away and crossed the street, relieved at last, to be looking away from her. There was nowhere to go to across the street but the large outdoor parking lot of the gym. Bob drove aimlessly, content to trace continuous figure eights in the parking lot.

"You seem nervous," she said. "Don't be. I assure you, there's nothing to worry about."

"Ms. Doyle," said Bob.

"Please, Shania. And may I call you Bob?"

"Sure, everyone else does."

"Good. Bob, I heard about your day. Quite an extraordinary day."

"Yes. It was that."

"I'd like to hear from you what happened. Can you walk me through it?"

"No, I can't. I'm sorry."

"Why not, Bob?" She put her hand on his arm.

"Ms. Doyle, Shania, I'm a private person by nature. What happened yesterday was out of the ordinary. Unforeseeable. My fear is that it may bring unintended consequences that may affect my low profile existence."

"You give me too much credit, Bob. It's just a community news piece."

"I really would rather you found a different story."

"Oh? Like what? There is no other story here. There's only one story and it's you, Bob. Hero Maintenance Man Saves Three. What, are you afraid I'll make you famous?"

Bob was still meandering in slow figure eights through the parking lot.

"Look, I can't tell you why, but I have a good reason for wanting to stay under the radar here, well under the radar."

"Are you a wanted man?"

"I'm not a criminal."

"Let's see, not a criminal. Are you in the Witness Protection Program?"

Bob's foot involuntarily hit the brake.

"Oh, sorry," he said. "Of course not."

"Struck a nerve there?"

"No. My foot slipped."

"Who's after you, then?"

Bob clenched his jaw to keep his mouth shut.

"Bob, I just got this job," she said. "I come back empty handed, and I'm back in the Food Section." Her lip curled in a childish pout.

"You'll get another shot," said Bob.

She smiled the pout away. "Yeah, I will."

"Shania, it's been a rare pleasure," said Bob. He turned the cart back toward the Lodge, but she touched his arm and pointed to a red Mazda in the visitor's lot. "That's me."

He drove to her car, and she slid her card into his shirt pocket. "Call me," she said. "I want to know how this turns out."

Bob nodded. He could not get away from her fast enough. She stepped back toward him, as if intending to give him a farewell peck on the cheek, but instead, she touched his neck gently, took a grip on his collar and looked deep into his eyes. He tried to look away, but could not.

"Who else knows?" she whispered. "Anybody?"

Bob gulped. No pithy bon mot sprang to mind.

She released him, kissed her first two fingers and touched them to his cheek. She smiled and made the hand sign of a phone ringing in her ear. "Call me," she mouthed.

Bob drove the cart back to the shop, thoroughly frazzled.

CHAPTER SIX
FLYSPECK

Behind the door to the front desk and reception area, in the tiny nucleus of the hotel, Constance occupied the second of the three offices with doors. Those three offices faced a short hallway crowded with a copy machine and a staff mail closet at one end and an open area in the back where Joanne, the PBX operator, answered the phone and dispatched radio calls.

The code number 50 identified all Lodge transmissions. "Fifty to Maintenance" was a call to Bob, or to any maintenance man with a radio.

Joanne, a dark-haired, sassy retiree with a Long Island accent, was also a member of the Lodge and Club. She didn't need her part-time job in quite the same sense that most employees needed their medical benefits and were willing to endure all to keep them, and definitely not enough to kowtow to Constance. She had other income and had taken the job because she liked to stay busy and keep her mind occupied. Answering the phone was easy enough. She kept a novel handy by her desk and read whenever things were slow, knowing full well how it grinded on Constance to see her sitting there at her desk reading a novel instead of finding something else to do.

Joanne's job was to answer the phone. At the moment, the phone was not ringing.

Constance stood over her, looking down. She didn't have to say a word, or even raise an eyebrow. All her thoughts were written on her face.

Joanne knew her days were numbered. The last year at the Lodge had been a bloodbath. A lot of employees had been let go, and all had seen their hours reduced. The economy had taken a hard hit, and the hotel business felt it.

"What?" said Joanne, looking up from her book.

As a mere supervisor, not a department head, Constance was not authorized to close and lock her office door, yet she did so frequently. She had her own auxiliary transmitter and could monitor radio calls, hit a bypass button and broadcast to maintenance from her office.

Joanne's whole workstation could easily be eliminated. And it would be.

"Please redirect any calls from the Senator's room to my office. Can you do that?"

"Certainly," said Joanne. "Anything else?"

"No, you can get back to your book."

Constance retreated to her office and closed the door.

A cruel rumor was widely believed, that Constance was blowing her boss, Dick Skinner, the front desk manager.

As a rule, the door to his windowless corner office was kept closed and locked.

The third and smallest office was a community work station filled with stacks of electronic equipment and a single computer desk. The door to that office was seldom, if ever, closed during the day. Dick Skinner was in there, resetting the Lodge home page for the cable televisions in the guest rooms.

When he had finished, he knocked on Constance's door, checked the handle, and opened her door enough to poke his head into her office and ask her to come to his office.

Constance followed Dick past Joanne's desk and into his office. Nothing was soundproof in those small rooms, not to the pitch of That Bitch's voice.

Taking an insouciantly derisive tone, Constance said, "Yes, your maleness?"

"Stop, all right?" said Dick. "It's not that big a deal."

"You're right. It's not … that big a …"

"I said stop."

"Stop? That's your 'safe' word? Stop? How original."

Constance's laugh was a fluttering twinkle.

Dick cut it short. "A Mr. Featherington checked in last night. You gave him a family discount."

"He's my great uncle."

"A billionaire," said Dick. "Yes. I looked him up."

"All the more reason to give him a discount if he wants one."

"Why is his name different than yours if he's what, your grandfather's brother?"

Constance tsked, "Ask him."

"You might be an heiress," said Dick, with some new suavity in his voice that Joanne found more obnoxious than the novel she was reading.

Constance's professionally pleasant demeanor stayed frozen in place while her bantering tone remained airy and light, but the steel bite inside her words trailed in essence behind her like scent after she'd left Dick's office saying as she backed out the door, "Someday I may own this place and then I'll be your boss."

Constance closed Dick's office door behind her and looked over at Joanne, who kept her eyes discreetly lowered to the pages of her book, as if she had heard none of their conversation. A moment later, Constance closed the door to her own office.

Constance locked her office door and sat under the blowing AC vent over her desk and let it blast down on the top of her head until the part in her hair felt cold on her scalp. It did no good to complain about the temperature. Complaining earned you a reputation as a complainer, in addition to anything else they could stir up to say about her, like crude jokes about hot flashes.

Constance knew that she was not well liked. That didn't matter so much. It certainly didn't matter what Bob thought of her. Bob was just an annoying old man. The fact that she was obligated to interact with him at all was enough of an imposition. Each time she asked him nicely to regulate the temperature, he found a new way to imply that her request was unreasonable.

It was always too hot or too cold. A degree or two up or down could make all the difference in the world sometimes. Men like Bob didn't understand that. Or if they did, they acted like they wished they didn't.

Constance sat at her desk with an open file folder containing her personal collection of comment cards from guests who had written favorable, even laudatory remarks about her. *Constance was great – very helpful!* The handwriting on some of the cards was barely legible.

Constance's right hand danced across a practice pad, mimicking two different scrawls, *Constance was the consummate professional.* And *Constance made our stay at the Lodge a delight.* She wrote the sentences over and over in alternating handwriting styles as a fly buzzed around the room. With an orange plastic flyswatter, she took a left-handed slap at the fly.

Under a magnifying lens attached to her desk lamp she compared her practice samples to the original handwriting. Satisfied, she reached down and turned on the portable shredder. She let the sample sheets disappear into the shredder, closed the file of comment cards and re-filed them in a locked cabinet.

All the comments in her file were authentic. None had been forged or coerced out of clients. Constance was indeed a consummate professional, and the majority of her clients recognized that. Certain clients were incapable of recognizing quality.

The comment card collection should have been enough for her by itself. There was ample evidence of her professionalism in the genuine documents, but the strange temptation she felt to experiment with forgery had grown into a hobby. She had discovered a talent that could get her into trouble. She had never yet included any forged comment cards with the originals, and she harbored no intention to do so. It was an aberration to continue practicing, now that she knew she had the skill to mimic almost any handwriting. It was a knack she had discovered and sharpened, a talent she secretly enjoyed. She was not planning to cross the line from dangerous hobby to stupid crime, but it gave her an odd sense of loss to shred her creations.

The large AC vent over her desk kicked on again and blew a blast of cold air down on the top of her head. She picked up her phone and dialed the maintenance shop extension.

The voice she expected came on the line. "Good morning, Maintenance. This is Bob."

"Bob," she said, "Could you please adjust the temperature back here so it's a little less cold?"

"Less cold," said Bob.

"It's freezing back here. And the AC vent, as you know, is directly above my head."

"Yes, a questionable desk placement. But you know, it would be easier to move your desk than it would be to move the air vent."

"Bob," Constance sighed, "I'm not asking you to move the air vent. Can't you just bump it up a little?"

"And when it starts getting warmish in the lobby, say, in about an hour, you can call me back, and I'll turn it back down a degree."

"You know, Bob, you don't have to try so hard to be so glib all the time."

"Glib? *Moi?*"

"Maybe you shouldn't try so hard."

"Maybe we should agree to say as little as possible to each other."

"Fine with me," she said and hung up.

The fly landed on her computer screen. Constance tensed her left forearm like a predator poised to strike. She swatted the fly and left its carcass a blotch on the monitor screen. She flicked it with a fingernail and watched it slide down the screen and drop to the tabletop behind her keyboard. She tore off a piece of scotch tape from the dispenser on her desk and picked the dead fly up with the sticky middle. She carried the flyspeck to the wall by the door and stuck it to the right of the light switch. Then she took a fine tip pen and wrote *Bob* on the wall and drew a tiny arrow pointing to the dead fly.

CHAPTER SEVEN
THE SPEARHEAD

Senator James Turner Rutland lay back in his suite's luxurious tub. He no longer smoked or drank, which made luxuriating in a tub without a cigar or a drink seem pointless. He had given up those habits after his stroke. The truth was he still had the desire to smoke and the will to drink to excess. It was only a matter of time before his resolve eroded.

He soaked in the tub with the warm jets circulating until the time had come to let the water out of the tub and get out. He dried off with a big bath towel in front of the mirror and flexed his chest once in shame. He donned and belted the white terrycloth robe with the embroidered seashell logo of the Lodge on the pocket and put on the matching slippers provided. He looked at himself in the mirror and saw a man ready to die.

He looked deeper into the caverns of his eyes and saw that there were things to do yet. No need to get morbid.

He picked up the remote and clicked on the flat screen tv. When the picture came up, he clicked it off. He tossed the remote on the bed and reached for the phone. He dialed the front desk and told Constance there was a problem with the remote.

She promised to have it taken care of.

"I tell you, I heard about this Bob fellow," said Senator Rutland. "Is he here today? I'd like to meet him."

"I'll see if I can find him," said Constance.

"Thank you, Connie."

James T. Rutland sat on the edge of the bed and leaned back on the pile of pillows. He opened the battery compartment of the remote, turned one battery to the opposite pole, closed the compartment and placed the remote on the bedside table.

He still had no pants on under the robe when he heard the tap on the door and the word, "Maintenance," announced from outside the room.

"Just a sec," he called back, sliding off the bed to slip on a pair of shorts. He re-tied the robe around his waist, unlocked the door and opened it.

There stood Bob of the Lodge, crisp as a biscuit in his maintenance uniform, dark blue pants and light blue shirt with an embroidered seashell logo and a gold colored nametag over the pocket that read *Bob*. A two-way radio hung from his hip next to a Gerber handy tool.

"Senator Rutland, I presume."

"Hello, Bob," said the Senator. "Please come in."

Bob crossed the threshold. "Having a little trouble with the remote?"

"That blasted thing," said the Senator. "I took the batteries out and put them back in, but it still won't work."

Bob found the remote and deftly replaced both batteries with new ones. The remote responded and he left the TV on.

"Thanks so much," said J. T. Rutland, clicking it off again. "I probably had them in backwards."

"Easy to do with triple A's; they're so small," said Bob. He smiled and took a step backward toward the door. "Is there anything else I can do for you today?"

Rutland returned the smile. "You look good, Bob. What did you lose, fifty, sixty pounds?"

Bob did not respond right away. "You may have me confused with someone else."

Rutland's head cocked a slight degree, as if considering a possible error.

"I study people, Bob. It's a lifelong habit. The way a person walks is like a signature, very difficult to change or disguise. Your walk reveals certain aspects of your character. Your walk, Bob, reflects a deliberate steadiness, a sense of relentlessness, if you will. You walk sort of like a wind-up toy, except you don't wear down. Your pace is constant. Fluid, yet it looks almost mechanical, like you're counting steps."

"I don't count steps," said Bob.

"Bob, there's a lot of dirty laundry in the State of Alabama. You know that as well as I do. I came to warn you because I knew you were here. I figure we owe you a heads up, at the very least, if nothing else."

"Are you the bearer of bad tidings?"

"I am, Bob. But I'm on your side. You and me, Bob. We put that Wilhoite sumbitch away once."

"I don't recall your role in all that, Senator," said Bob.

"Don't recall my role? Bob, I spearheaded that whole megilla. The statewide anti-corruption drive? That was my baby. Bingo machines. Hell, we had to nail him on something. White slavery, murder for hire, drugs. Umpteen witnesses disappeared. We blindsided him with that trucking angle, thanks to you. Interstate transport of gambling equipment. People laugh about it, even today, but we got him. Took down ever damn bingo hall in the state, too."

"He still only got five years. It's been four. Who let him out?"

"That's what I came to tell you, Bob. Larry Wilhoite's been a model prisoner. He was paroled four days ago."

Bob resisted the urge to sit down. "I should have been notified in advance."

"Frankly, Bob, I find it grave cause for concern that you were not."

"Are you privy to the particulars of my situation?"

"Absolutely not. I was aware that you were threatened, as was I, as were others. We've seen witnesses disappear before. It's not uncommon. So, when you dropped off the radar, certain people put two and two together and said you must have taken a powder, set out for parts unknown, or were quite possibly dead, but the smart money guessed you went with WitSec. And, you know, more power to you. This is a nice place to hide out. I'd be a little worried, though, after that stunt yesterday, saving all those people. I'd be wondering if maybe my low-profile days weren't numbered around here. How'd your interview go with that reporter, by the way?"

"You're really plugged in, aren't you?"

"You're the talk of the town, Bob."

"She also claims to be on my side. What do you think?"

"Bob, five years ago, if we had had anything stronger to hang on Wilhoite than moving bingo machines across state lines, we would have jumped over a bunch of frogs to do it. He's a slippery devil. I don't know what to tell you. It's all so sordid. Have a drink with me, Bob. I'll tell you some shit that will curl your hair."

"So," said Bob, "politics is sordid."

"Bob, I drink heavily," said Rutland. "Have for years. Quite often I find I no longer enjoy total recall. I wake up in strange places, embarrassed, with strange women and no memory of what I may have said or done. I have, of course, tried rehab. I'm nine days sober right now."

"Congratulations."

"Thank you. But I'm ready to jump off the stagecoach any minute. Have one with me, Bob. You don't want me on your conscience."

"I'm on the clock, Senator."

"Good one. I like that. Bob, it's been real and it's been good, but, as they say, it hasn't been real good talking with you. If you don't mind my saying so, you're not putting two and two together here real quick."

"Did you tell anyone you saw me here?" Bob asked.

"Bob, there's a black book of names that will answer all your questions."

"How about one question?" said Bob.

"Good God, man, what do you think? Would you trust a drunk with confidential information? He'll find you here. Him, they. Your only hope is to run."

"I'm not running," said Bob.

"They'll kill you. They don't mind."

Bob heard the summons from the radio on his belt, "Fifty to Maintenance."

He responded to Constance, "Go ahead Fifty."

"Bob are you still in 433?"

Bob took his time to answer. "Affirmative."

"Please call me on the room phone."

Bob clipped the radio back to his belt. He looked at the Senator, who was smiling at him slyly.

J. T. Rutland said, "That Connie's a sweetheart."

"What do you want from me, Senator? You didn't come here just to warn me. I don't believe that."

"I wouldn't believe it, either. No reason why you should."

"What, then?"

"I want to make a deal with you."

"Not interested," said Bob. He picked up the Senator's bedside phone and dialed Constance's extension.

Constance picked up immediately and said, "Bob, how long does it take to fix a remote? What in the world are you doing in there?"

"The Senator and I were having a chat," said Bob. "Politics, world affairs, things of that nature."

"Hanging out with guests in their rooms is not included in your job description," she cautioned him. "You are aware of that, aren't you?"

"Just going the extra mile," said Bob. He hung up the phone and turned back to the Senator.

"She's warm for you, Bob," said Rutland.

Bob ignored that observation. "What kind of deal?"

"Y'all have this Hepburn and Tracy thing happening."

"No, we don't," said Bob.

"The kind of deal where you testify again, and this time he goes down for good."

"Absolutely not," said Bob.

CHAPTER EIGHT
WORLDS IN COLLISION

Throughout the long afternoon, while Bob responded to radio calls from Housekeeping, he thought of nothing but what he would say to Berne Ventine later when he called.

Shower drains clogged, faucets dripped, toilets plugged. Curtain rods needed hooks and sliders. Various light bulbs needed replacement.

Back in the maintenance shop at the end of the day shift, the last half hour eked by like a glacier.

Karl attempted to regale Bob with an account of Nestor the Albanian cook, whom Bob had nicknamed Vlad, to which Karl had added the embellishment, Normally Taciturn.

"Normally Taciturn Vlad," said Karl, "was hopped up on ecstasy or something, hitting on waitresses in the dining room, leaning his elbows on the maitre'd's podium, laughing and joking, cutting up. He suddenly turned into Vlad the Outgoing."

Bob's lips were closed on a tight half grimace.

"Vlad has seen me almost every day now for five years," said Karl, "walking around in painter whites, and we've never spoken more than a word or two to at any time to each other in passing: hello, good morning, nothing more. So he comes up to me today and says, 'Hey, Karl. You're the painter, yes?'"

Stories told in the maintenance shop often were created from nothing, went nowhere and had no point, other than to alleviate the crushing, soul-sucking tedium. The story Karl was telling about Vlad was one of those. It was probably going to end up with Karl agreeing to paint Vlad's house.

Bob silently willed Karl to wrap it up, get to the end, stop talking and move on. He didn't want to have to listen anymore. He just wanted to go home.

There were moments when the air in the shop was too close for conversation, too starved of energy to pretend otherwise, or, at the other extreme, too charged with tension to concede an inch of space to the niceties of social interaction. Always the alpha dog in the room set the tone, himself at his desk with his paperwork, the former Master Chief of the Navy, Edwin Nogg.

Bob and Ed could talk to each other about anything work-related and never stray into personal zones. Bob and Ed were at ease with each other. Having served in the Navy, Bob knew how to anchor their working relationship within the bounds of military camaraderie.

Karl had no such ability. It took all his reserves of guile to feign a passing interest in maintenance issues unrelated to painting. Ed Nogg did not respect that attitude. He wanted everyone to be more like Bob.

Ed and Karl clashed.

The maintenance shop was too cramped and small to accommodate ego collisions. Karl had to bow, and bow he did. He had worked hard for many years at his own specific trade so as not to be saddled with another. Yet little by little, Ed required Karl to perform more maintenance oriented tasks in addition to an undiminished list of paint-related demands.

Behavior modification was in play at all times. The daily lists of tasks, the relentless generation of lists, the accumulation of tasks upon tasks, the stress, the absurdity of unreasonable expectations, impossible missions undertaken and completed, the small triumphs of perfection and of near-perfection, the quiet trade of secret knowledge; the maintenance shop was a sanctuary, a hall of tools, a place where work of all kinds was accomplished, where things were built. Men worked here. They clashed and moved on.

Karl and Ed could fume like chimneys, each in an opposite end of the shop, sharing a small space, Ed at his desk, eyes deep in paperwork and Karl at his paint table, standing, pretending to occupy his time with organizational matters; cleaning tools, planning projects, anything to keep from revealing any outward signs of sloth.

Karl's respect for Ed notwithstanding, he had never served in the military and did not respond well to Ed's military style. Karl's history included decades of self-employment. In his view, as long as he was painting and his work was excellent, then nothing more should be expected of him, certainly not adherence to any military code of conduct or any psychological obeisance to authority.

Karl and Ed were respectfully not friends, not like Bob and Ed were friends, nor, by any stretch, like Karl and Bob were friends. In the shop, Bob served as a buffer zone between Karl and Ed. Without Bob, they would have clashed harder, and Karl would not have survived as an employee for five years.

There were times when Bob felt pressured by the demands of workplace friendships.

As he drove homeward it mattered less if the glass was half-full or half-empty.

At five o'clock, Berne Ventine called Bob at home. Bob had showered by then and was sitting at his desk with a drink and the phone an inch from his hand when it rang. Caller ID showed encrypted blankness on the LED, signaling a call from a USMS secure line.

Bob picked up the phone on the first ring. "I consider your dereliction of duty an egregious breach of trust," said Bob.

"Whoa," said Berne Ventine. "Whoa down. Let me explain something to you. I knew Wilhoite was up for parole, and I wanted to tell you, but I was specifically instructed not to."

"By whom?"

"You know I can't tell you that. It was decided that the parole hearing would proceed unencumbered."

"Favors owed," said Bob.

"It's a little more complicated than that," said Berne.

"Is it? So when did you plan to tell me?"

"I didn't have to tell you at all. It's not any part of my job to keep you in the loop. Periodic updates, sure, yeah, but things change from day to day. Some things you don't need to know. Some things no one needs to know."

"Like am I or am I not on a hit list?"

"What did the Senator say about that?"

"Why should I tell you? So you can tell your masters?"

"Bob, you don't want to go through this alone."

"Go through what? What exactly is my status? What am I filed under? B for Bait?"

"No, Bob. B is still for Bob."

"Don't joke, Berne. You know I'm being dangled. I am alligator bait.

You know it, and I know it, and the Senator knows it. And just because there are twenty field agents watching over me doesn't mean I ever consented to be dangled like a hamhock over a swamp."

"It's not like that, Bob. The Senator had no clearance to talk to you about this."

"There's a black book of names in the mix, too," said Bob.

"What exactly did the Senator say about that?"

"Just that there is one. Does that shithead, Wilhoite, have it? What, has he got you all over a barrel with some shoddy little book of indiscretions? Is this the U.S. Justice Department and the Marshals Service cowering at the parole hearing of a common gangster?"

"Bob, this is bigger than Larry the Cherry. This is the dark hole of big. This is the Dixie Mafia's connection to the halls of power. Yes, there's a black book, but it's not just a shoddy little book of indiscretions filled with some hooker's list of clients. This is the mother lode."

"Spare me. You can't handle this without me?"

"Bob, your cover's blown. It's time to fold your tent. The Senator has a big mouth. You have been compromised."

"You don't know that, for sure, though do you? You actually have no idea what Wilhoite might have said about me or to whom?"

"That's correct, unfortunately."

"The Senator asked me to come back to Mobile. He said they were going to try Larry Wilhoite for murder, and that I could be called to testify against him again."

"That's an undeveloped scenario. There's no case against him yet, not for murder."

"Unless he kills me?"

"Well, then, yeah. Then we'd have him cold."

"But you still wouldn't have the black book."

"Also correct."

"So what's the plan?"

"Bob, did I ever tell you I was in charge of making plans? Did you ever really think that I was that guy? How wrong you would be, my friend, were you to ever think such a thing. No, Bob, I follow instructions. I try not to fuck things up any worse than they already are, but the plans come to me half-baked and doomed and always, always fucked up in some major way. It's not my doing. It's never my plan. Bob, I do not want you to get hurt. I'm committed to that, but I'm trying to do my job at the same time."

"Berne, I don't care about the big dark hole. Law enforcement or the greater good. I just want to live out the rest of my little life without changing my name again. I'd like to not repeat that ordeal. All I want I have right now. A job, a truck, an apartment. An identity. I'm not giving any of it up. If he comes, he comes. I've got a gun."

"Well, then, Cowboy Bob, I hope you see him coming," said Berne.

CHAPTER NINE
HOME ON THE RANGE

Bob loaded his gun kit and drove to the shooting range.

Wrung out from the day's events, he fitted the sound suppressing pads over his ears and fired off a couple of rounds, shredding the outer edges of the targets. He checked his breathing, re-addressed his stance and tried to clear his mind of clutter and focus his concentration on nothing other than the black dot in the central ring of the target. He emptied the clip, ejected it and loaded another.

By the third clip, his nerves settled down. A vein of icy calm began to flow between his hand and eye. The bullet holes in the targets narrowed until he was shredding the central rings.

"Quite respectable." The light touch on his left arm startled him. Shania Doyle stood beside him in a black leather jacket and faded jeans, near enough to whisper or slide a dagger between his ribs.

He removed his ear protection, suddenly certain that he had never been watchful or wary enough of dangerous people.

"You look like you're ready to kill someone," she said.

Her smile melted what remained of his icy calm. She smiled like they were old friends. "Come on, Bob. I'm not stalking you."

"Note to self," said Bob, "update street skills."

The polished walnut box in her hands looked heavy.

"What did you bring?" Bob cleared a space on the counter, and she set the box down. A dark weathered wood inlaid with silver and turquoise trim, the box looked old and Mexican.

She opened it and showed him an antique pearl-handled gunfighter pistol. "Yeah. That's right. A Peacemaker."

"Strap that to your leg, do you?"

She picked the pistol up and spun it on her finger. "Hey, I'm Hannie Caulder, baby."

Bob had a sensation then of falling forward into an infinite chasm and submerging in deep green depths and roiling upward through amniotic fluid and rising out of breath into a Baja sun-bleached sky over a desert beach by a hacienda where, in a din of gunfire and shattering empty whiskey bottles, Raquel Welch in a serape learns from Bob Culp, the sad-eyed old gunfighter, how to shoot to kill. Bob, in the lengthening moment of his fall, neither noted nor cared that he was not Bob Culp; it could have been him in that movie teaching Hannie Calder how to shoot, except for the shoot to kill part.

"It belonged to my grandfather," said Shania.

Bob stepped to one side, offering her the spot. "Shoot," he said. He could not wipe the grin from his face. Every early warning signal in his sixty-one-year-old circuitry was snapping, crackling and popping, firing off signal flares over synapses dormant for decades singing out like sentries spotting threats on all horizons.

There was no way back to the life he'd led last week, the quiet, uneventful evenings, the freedom of anonymity. No more waiting and wondering if hiding was better than fighting, living better than dying. The hiding was ending, at last, the difference clear: now his life had turned serious. The question of whether or not he could shoot to kill was no longer hypothetical. There was every reason to believe he would be tested.

Shania loaded six chambers, rolled the cylinder like she had seen done in a thousand movies, adjusted her ear protection and took a two-handed aim at a paper target. Bob had his ear protection back on when the shot rang out.

Shania lowered the 45. "Wow."

"Guess I'll be moseyin' on," said Bob.

"Stay awhile, Bob," she said.

"Okay."

"Watch me shoot."

Bob watched her shoot. He watched every inch of her coil and flex and recoil as she shot that big pistol.

A kind of intimacy derives from not talking, even without gunfire.

While she shot, there was no need for them to talk. Bob watched her. She'd been well taught. When she was finished, the talking began again, but a moment more intimate than talk had passed between them.

"So what brings you out here tonight?" she asked.

"Just a whim," said Bob.

"But why tonight? Isn't it late?"

"Late for me, you mean?"

"I didn't mean it quite like that, but yeah. Is this how you spend your Friday nights?"

"Is this how you spend yours?"

They were walking out to the parking lot and came to his truck first.

"Good night, Bob," said Shania. "Nice to see you out and about."

Bob drove home wondering what she had meant by that. Did she think he was a stay-at-home, a never-leave-the-porch old guy? Or was it just something she said without thinking, without trying to layer on another level of meaning, like sugar frosting slathered on a brownie, overcompensation for insecurity. Best not to think about her at all.

As if that was going to happen.

In the morning, he woke to a memory of Shania wielding her big Peacemaker. He heated water on the stovetop for a bowl of instant oatmeal and pictured himself offering Shania a bowl and the look on her face as she declined. He poured hot water into the Honey Maple flavored bowl of mush and stirred, imagining himself telling her, "It's very good. You should try some."

A puff of steam rose from the bowl. Bob dumped the contents in the sink, turned on the water and ran the oatmeal down the drain.

CHAPTER TEN
STAND DOWN

Bob's normal day off was Saturday, but he was always willing to cover an extra shift. He drove to work, backed his truck into the slot facing the exit, opened the shop, unplugged the battery charger from the golf cart and backed the cart out through the double doors. He put on a pot of coffee, checked Ed's email inbox for urgent messages, then made his way to the front desk to pick up the current paperwork and maybe schmooze with the Queen. But no, in the parking garage, he noticed Constance's faded red MG in her slot. She must have worked the late shift and would be getting off soon, thought Bob. Or she had come in early for some reason.

Constance stood behind the front desk, every shellacked blonde hair in place. Karl had nicknamed her Marianne Faithfull, though it didn't stick. "She smiles like a jaded groupie," he said. Karl had her pegged as a wanton with a Daddy complex and discipline issues.

None of her nicknames were adequate. Marianne Faithfull had devolved to Marianne Faithless and further to Shop-Vac before rebounding to the less unkind generic, Thunderthighs.

It was immature, cruel, and wrong on every level, not to mention a clear transgression of employee sensitivity training, to besmirch her character with unkind nicknames, and Bob, on principle, took no pride in the baser instincts that drove him to make sport of her behind her back. He regretted the behind her back part, which had since been rectified. Their hostilities now were unconcealed. His intent with Constance now was to goad her to a froth whenever possible, while remaining nonplussed.

Bob did this not merely because he could but because she deserved it. And because she had asked for it.

By midmorning, the Scottish housekeeper, Catherine, had pushed her cart to the Senator's door twice, knocked and called out several times with no answer. The second time, around nine-thirty; she heard an electronic alarm beeping inside the room. It was still beeping as she called through the door again, "Haesekeeping."

Bob exited a nearby room, and Catherine waved him down. Outside the Senator's door, she said, "Mister Bob, isnae right in tha. Gives mae the willies. Creeps mae."

The lilt in her voice had come all the way from Edinburgh, but the last time she'd gone home, her oldest friends had teased her about losing her accent. They told her she sounded like an American redneck.

Bob knocked and announced "Maintenance," three times before he used his key card to unlock the unit. He took a step inside and called out, "Hello, Maintenance."

Catherine held back outside the door. She'd been at the Lodge eleven years, and nothing had ever spooked her before. But she didn't want to go in.

The blinds were drawn across the patio doors, and the bathroom door was closed. The room was dark. The bed looked slept in. Otherwise, the room was neat.

Bob knocked on the bathroom door, called out and heard nothing. He opened the bathroom door and saw himself in the big mirror over the vanity sinks. He saw on its marginal periphery a color reflected that didn't belong.

One step to his right was the tub, full to the Senator's armpits with red, red water.

Bob unclipped his radio and called, "Maintenance to Fifty-call 911."

Constance answered, "Fifty, go ahead."

Rooted in the middle of the bathroom floor, Bob did not move his feet as he took in the details of the scene.

"Did you call 911 yet?" he asked.

"And tell them what?" Her tone came across the air as peevish.

"Request detectives. 433 is a crime scene."

"Bob, what have you done?" Constance sighed. "What are you doing?"

Bob took another look around. Nothing was apparently awry outside the tub. The marble tiles were clean and dry. Spotless. No puddles or footprints on the floor but his own.

He decided not to take another step.

Inside the tub, the Senator's wrists were both submerged. The razor cuts on his wrists were not visible through the opaque bloody water. Bob could not say with certainty that the Senator had not bled out from some other slashed artery, but the way of the old Roman senators was to cut the wrists. Open a vein, bleed out in the bath. Both wrists. To die from one cut took too long. The second cut showed you were serious, in control of your destiny, enough to choose the noble grandeur of the Roman tradition.

The bath mat was out of place, spread neatly under the vanity sinks instead of in the middle of the floor, not an accidental placement. The floor where Bob was standing had been wiped clean and dry.

The blood was all contained inside the tub, but splash marks showed as pale pink drip stains on the marble walls, and above the marble backsplash on the peach-colored painted walls. Even on the gray stained tongue in groove paneled wood ceiling were discolored traces of bloody water splash.

But the Senator did not look like he had died splashing. He looked like he had bled out in peace as he had intended.

Bob took a careful step backward and one more look around and then he was out of the bathroom. He retraced his steps out of the suite and closed the front door.

Catherine was gone.

He leaned on the railing outside the room and waited. Across the boulevard in the Belle Rive Realty Office parking lot, a crew of nine groundskeepers was trimming palm trees, mowing and edging the lawn, landscaping, planting perennials, raking, sweeping, running leaf blowers. Life went on.

Bob had less than a minute to decide what to do. The sound of a multitude of keys jangling on Marvin Gardener's belt loop announced the arrival of the Head of Security, walking a half step faster than usual, his keys clashing to accelerated rhythm.

Bob held a palm forth to slow his advance. "Marvin, we need to keep everyone out of this room. It's a crime scene."

Marvin read as much as he could from Bob's face. Then he asked, "What happened?"

"Let's get a detective down here and find out," said Bob.

Marvin pulled his radio out and called his network supervisor.

"Hang on, Bob," said Marvin. "I'll get a detective. Sit tight."

Bob remained where he was, leaning against the railing. He watched Marvin walk a short way off then double back.

"Bob, the EMTs are en route. They need to make the call whether or not the Senator's dead. That's just SOP, standard operating procedure. Trust me, you don't want that responsibility."

"I'll talk to them," said Bob.

"I know how these things go," said Marvin. "You could get caught in the middle of a giant shit storm. Excuse my French."

Catherine returned with Irina, the Czech housekeeper.

"What happen, Mister Bob?" Irina asked.

"Tell us," said Catherine.

"It's a police matter," said Bob. "I can't tell you anything."

"Is he dead innae?" said Catherine.

"Now's not the time, Catherine," said Marvin. "You ladies need to scoot."

"He dead?" said Irina. "Dead?"

"Shh," said Catherine, pulling her away, "come on, Irina."

A fire truck parked on the street in front of the building, an ambulance behind it.

Marvin headed down to meet them. He escorted two firemen and two EMTs to the elevator. They came to the fourth floor and advanced down the corridor to talk to Bob outside the door to 433.

One of the firemen shook Bob's hand and introduced himself as the Chief. "We'll take it from here," he said.

"There's nothing an EMT can do at this point for the senator," said Bob. "The police need to see this crime scene first."

The Fire Chief cocked his ear to the door. The alarm was still beeping.

"What's that?"

"His watch," said Bob.

"People revive you never think they will. Happens all the time."

"I'm asking you," said Bob, "to preserve a crime scene."

The Fire Chief looked at Bob's name tag. "Bob, are you in charge of the Maintenance Department?"

"At the moment."

"You have no authority to ask us to stand down."

"It's the right thing to do," said Bob.

"Not your call. A man's life hangs in the balance, and you refuse him certified medical care, you're held accountable for his death. How's that sound?"

"The man's dead," said Bob. "There's no question."

"Appearances can be deceiving. You're sticking your neck out. For what?"

A Belle Rive County Sheriff's Deputy pulled his patrol car into the lot and parked in front of the fire truck, blocking the exit.

The Fire Chief looked at Bob and nodded. "All right, Bob. We'll stand down."

CHAPTER ELEVEN
ROLL TIDE

Detective Billy Carlisle had solved one headline murder case and worked on several others. In tiny Belle Rive County, that had made him top dog in a one-dog town.

Several years ago, a waitress at a popular restaurant was found strangled in her apartment. Clues in her financial records led the detective to conclude she was supporting a deadbeat ex-boyfriend who was a massive consumer of steroids.

Detective Billy Carlisle made the front page on that one. The ex-boyfriend confessed. She had cut him off and tried to move on without him, without factoring in to her decision how much he loved her or how badly she was hurting him. His plan to scare some sense into her had gone awry, and he was mortally sorry after he killed her. The "Roid Rage Killer" was convicted and hung himself in prison.

Since then, Detective Carlisle had represented Belle Rive County on several statewide task forces, but homicides were still highly uncommon among the rarefied constituency he was pledged to protect and serve.

The detective wore a light tan jacket over a taupe V-neck tee. He checked his reflection in the rearview mirror, winked at himself and slipped on his shades. He swung around and stepped out as the Head of Lodge Security walked up, jangling his keys.

"Good morning, Billy."

"How do, Marvin. What seems to be the problem?"

"Well, our lead maintenance man, Bob, found one of our VIP guests dead in the room. Senator Rutland of Alabama."

"Is the death confirmed?"

"Fire Chief and the EMTs are waiting on you."

"How do we know he's really dead?"

"Bob said he is."

Detective Carlisle looked up at the bald old man with glasses watching him from the upper floor railing.

Marvin guided the detective to the elevator.

Bob waited with the firemen and the EMTs outside room 433. The detective shook hands with the Fire Chief before turning to Bob with a testy look.

"Hello, Bob," he said. "Watch a lot of CSI, do you?"

"I prefer NCIS," said Bob.

"Well," said Detective Carlisle, "just so you understand that this is the real thing, not some TV show."

"Words to live by," said Bob.

The detective appraised Bob more closely. "I suppose I should thank you for preserving my crime scene."

"You're welcome," said Bob.

Detective Carlisle fit paper footies over his shoes.

"What did you see in there?"

"A couple of things," said Bob. "The bathroom floor is bone dry, wiped clean."

"That strikes you as odd?"

"Combined with bloody splash marks on the walls and ceiling, yes."

"Bloody splash marks," the detective repeated. "I'll keep an eye peeled."

Bob used his key card to unlock the door. He pushed it open, and Detective Carlisle stepped inside.

"Wait here," said the detective.

The Fire Chief said, "I can't tell if you've made a friend or an enemy."

"Fifty to Maintenance." Bob grimaced at the sound of Constance's voice and unclipped his radio from his belt.

"Go ahead, Fifty."

"What's going on? Call me."

"I can't right now," said Bob. He turned the radio off and clipped it back to his belt.

Marvin said, "I'll go down and fill her in."

Detective Carlisle stepped outside. He addressed the Fire Chief, "Jimbo, y'all can go ahead on. I called techs."

"All right, Billy." The Fire Chief lifted his shoulders in a show of nonchalance. His eye caught Bob's. The EMTs and the other fireman followed him down the corridor to the elevator and out to their vehicles.

Detective Carlisle leaned on the railing next to Bob. "Well, Bob," he said, "it appears we have a situation here."

"Murder or suicide?" said Bob.

"Sure looks like suicide."

"Except for the dry floor and the splash marks," said Bob.

"Yeah, except for those anomalies," said the detective.

"Any ideas?"

"Not yet. You?"

"No. When I spoke with the Senator yesterday I heard no signs or indications of depression."

"Are you qualified to recognize such indications?"

"No more than anyone else."

"What did you and the Senator talk about?"

"Various things. Chit-chat. His remote wasn't working. I changed the batteries."

"What time was this?"

"Yesterday. Noonish."

"You were here in his room with him for how long, exactly?"

"Maybe half an hour."

"That's a long time, isn't it? For chit-chat and to fix a remote?"

"The Senator liked to talk. He must have thought I was a good listener."

"What did he talk about?"

"I don't know. Just talk. In one ear and out the other."

"I thought you were a good listener."

"I'm not, though. Not at all."

"Well, I'm going to need to interview every employee who had access to this room," said the detective.

"That would include housekeeping, maintenance, security, room service, management...happy hunting," said Bob.

"So be it," said the detective. "Bob, I'd like for you to try a little harder to remember your conversation with the Senator. It may be important."

"I wasn't paying much attention," said Bob.

The detective pulled out a pencil, as if he meant to take notes.

"Thirty minutes, that's a long conversation, not to remember any of it. What did y'all talk about? Sports, football, what?"

"Football, mostly," said Bob. "He kept saying 'Roll tide.' He was an ardent fan."

"How many times did he say, 'Roll tide'?"

"I didn't count."

The detective eyed Bob evenly. "What, did he just keep saying, 'roll tide, roll tide, roll tide?"

"Am I under suspicion?" Bob asked. "Am I a 'person of interest' here?"

"Bob," said the detective, "the way this works is, I'm in charge of asking questions. You're in charge of answering, or not answering. Call me Billy. I don't mind. Bob, you know, the truth is, there's nothing to be gained by broadcasting any of these private details we've discussed. I'm counting on you to keep what you've seen here to yourself."

"So, you're calling it a suicide," Bob said.

The detective snapped a card out of his coat pocket and handed it to Bob.

"Thanks for your help," he said. "I'll be in touch. Call me if you think of anything else."

CHAPTER TWELVE
SANCTUARY

Bob returned by the stairs to the sanctuary of the maintenance shop with a thousand-yard stare in place to deflect all possible inquiries. No one came near enough to ask him anything, but inquiring minds still wanted to know the gory details.

He expected to be asked some uncomfortable questions and had decided not to answer any of them. The best way to avoid having to craft disingenuous answers was to declare the entire subject off limits. He could hardly put forth on his own the proposition that the Senator's death was not a suicide. Not without asking for more trouble.

Control of the situation had passed from his hands into the capable hands of the county, Detective Carlisle, the lab techs and the medical examiner, none of whom were likely to dismiss as irrelevant the fact that an employee of the Lodge and Club had commandeered the crime scene. What was his rationale for that action?

Was he a trained detective? No.

Was it his intent to attract attention to himself? No. Attracting attention to himself ran counter to his *raison d'etre* as a ward of WitSec and hindered the mission of keeping a low profile and passing undetected under the radar.

Restating the obvious didn't make the glass any more full.

A killer was loose on the property. All other conclusions were secondary.

Bob had the maintenance shop to himself until two p.m. when his relief was scheduled to arrive for the evening shift. For a mere two hours their shifts overlapped and there were two regular maintenance men on duty. In all departments, including maintenance, cutbacks had reduced staff to skeletal levels.

Ed Nogg tried to spend most weekends with his wife, undisturbed, at home or fishing on his boat, leaving one maintenance man alone on the premises to cover the bulk of each shift. Bob took a small measure of pride in never having felt the need before to interrupt Ed Nogg's weekend with a phone call. Only respect for Ed and the obligation to warn him of the trouble he had brought to their horizon persuaded him to call him now.

Bob needed time to think. He had put everyone, guests, members and employees, at risk of unknown consequences, all because he wanted to keep his little job, his new identity, his secret little life. And one thing he knew already-even local media was more than he was prepared to handle.

Bob called Ed's cell and reached him on his boat.

Ed was already heading in. David had called him.

"Bob, I'm still an hour out," said Ed. "Hang loose in the shop. Don't take any calls. Don't answer the phone. Lock the door. You don't have to talk to anybody."

"I didn't call to ask you to come in," said Bob.

"I'm coming in," said Ed.

As soon as Bob hung up the phone, it rang. The Front Desk was calling, Constance with some new alarming concern. He let it go to message.

With or without him, rumors would circulate. Better without him, since no one, not even Bob, knew the truth about what had happened to the Senator.

However convinced he was that the Senator had been murdered, he was not even close to any other conclusions. At best, he could make an educated guess, that the Senator had been followed from Alabama, that he had led his own killer straight to the Lodge.

Was there any sign of Wilhoite? Surely, if he had a room, he would use a different name.

The assassin would have had access to a room. He'd stand out too much just hanging about. There were no loiterers at the Lodge.

Bob consulted the daily sheet and scanned the names of recent arrivals. One name leaped out at him. Featherington, R. P. in Room 431, two doors down from the Senator, had arrived Thursday evening and was booked to stay for three days. An assassin on a long weekend vacation? Doubtful, but the name, Featherington, so curiously similar to Constance's last name, Featherton; what to make of that, if anything?

Bob picked up the phone and punched in Constance's office extension. She answered on the second ring.

"Bob, thanks for calling me back. It's been like, an hour I've been calling you. I'm getting press inquiries, and I don't have any information at all. I need to know what's going on and you're the only one who knows, so could you please take that chip off your shoulder for one minute and tell me what's going on?"

Bob said, "Does the name Featherington mean anything to you?"

Constance took a moment to adjust the level of chill in her voice, "If you're referring to our guest, Bob, yes, he is a distant relative of mine. And no, I did not comp his room."

"How distant?" Bob asked.

"Not that it's any of your business. He's my grand uncle."

"Why is he here now?"

"Why does anyone come here, Bob?"

"Not to die, as a rule. Not to kill or be killed."

"Bob, on behalf of Lodge management, you are not our choice for press liaison."

"Good," said Bob. "You do it."

"Tell me one thing I can tell the press," said Constance. "Please."

Bob said, "I have no statement to make. I am incommunicado."

Bob hung up. What to make of the Featherington coincidence? Ten out of ten television detectives agreed that there was no such thing as coincidence.

Bob's pistol was in the glove box of his truck; he didn't bring it in.

Instead, he switched on the portable air compressor and went back to work. He checked the gauge and watched it rise to a hundred pounds of pressure. An ongoing shelf building project was underway on the workbench, a series of small shelves requiring a pneumatic nailer. That was the thing about the shop. There was every proper tool for every purpose near to hand, if you knew where to look and what to look for. And how to use the proper tool.

The televisions in all of the guest rooms were gradually being replaced with flat screen TVs, which fit differently inside the armoires, altering the placement of the DVD players attached. New shelves to hold new DVD players were being built to fit inside the old armoires and stained to match the pickled almond finish. Bob didn't worry about the stain or the finish. Karl would get to that. He just built the shelves. He had about fifty more to build.

When he was called away earlier, he had left the gun on the workbench, uncoupled from the air hose and loaded with 1.5-inch staples. In a fluid transition from brooding, Bob picked up the gun, attached it to the air hose and resumed his interrupted task. The sound of the compressor firing the nailer at regular intervals rang through the parking garage like an explosive heartbeat, signs of life from the maintenance shop.

The knock on the door was unthreatening, accompanied by a tentative "Hello."

An old man had walked up to the shop doors rolling a bicycle. He had heard the air compressor and wanted to know if he could pump up his tires with it.

"It won't take long," the old man said.

He was posed like a catalog model for *Senior Beachwear Quarterly* in matching Commodore beach jacket and trunks, with little anchor patterns on the jacket buttons and rope sandals, and one hand on the shiny blue beach cruiser like he was about to ride off on it.

Never too busy to help out a guest, Bob was about to uncouple the nail gun from the air hose and switch it with the tire nozzle and then proceed to check and fill the tires on the bike when some primal impulse warned him to wait. He did not uncouple the nail gun or set it down on the table. He carried it in his right hand and checked the old man's front tire with his left. The front tire didn't need air. The back tire didn't, either.

The old man was never going to ride that bicycle. He was pushing eighty, but he held himself like a gent from another era. With a dapper little smirk, he had a foot in the door already with the handlebars of the beach cruiser between himself and Bob, the front wheel pushing the door open.

"Sir," said Bob, "this part of the hotel is a restricted area."

The old man leaned the bike against the open door and stepped away from it into the shop. He wagged a finger at Bob. "Does that that nail gun have a safety feature?"

Bob took a step back.

"Reason I ask is most nail guns have safety features to prevent them from being fired from a distance, accidentally."

56

Bob fired into the back of the solid wood door from three feet away. A half inch of bent staple protruded from the white painted surface. "This one's been modified," he said.

"Relax, Mr. Deighton. Mr. Day. May I have a closer look at that nailer for a second?"

Behind the emptiness in his eyes, Bob sensed more than he saw of an infinite void. He raised the nail gun slowly until it pointed to the ceiling.

"What do you want?" Bob asked.

"What do you think I want?" The old man asked.

"In those togs, you want to be out by the pool, scoping chicks, don't you?" said Bob.

The old man grinned with his eyes. "I'm taking a break from all that young pussy."

"Not in here," said Bob.

"Are you going to shoot me with that nail gun?"

"There are two kinds of people in this world," said Bob, "those who won't ever shoot you with a nail gun, no matter what, and those who will."

The old man's laugh mocked Bob's bravado. "Can't you see the headline? MAINTENANCE MAN SHOOTS GUEST WITH NAIL GUN. How will that look in your grandson's scrapbook? There goes his inheritance. I'll ruin you."

Bob leveled the nailer at the old man's chest. The old man didn't flinch. When Bob pointed it at his eye, he flinched, but emptiness still covered his face like a mask.

The old man brushed aside the threat of the nail gun from a distance. "Put that thing away," he said.

Bob lowered it from the old man's face to his chest.

"My name is Featherington, Raleigh Featherington," said the old man.

Bob asked, "Who came first, the Featheringtons or the Feathertons?"

Featherington took the question in stride. "Featheringtons, of course," he said. "My brother, Daryl, was the first Featherton. He changed his name and moved to Wimauma to get away from me. Fifteen miles down the road, hardly outside my sphere of influence."

Bob asked, "Are you with Wilhoite's band of savages?"

"Larry? That bungler. Hell no. He's with me."

"What do you want?" Bob repeated.

Featherington showed a full set of teeth too perfect for his wizened skull.

"I don't have all day to horse around with you. Jimmy Rutland said you have my ledger."

Bob asked, "When did he say that?"

"With his last breath."

"What were his exact words?"

"He said, 'Bob has it.'"

Bob said, "He lied."

"I find it unimaginable that my old friend would utter a falsehood to me at such a time. Jimmy was like a son to me. Him and Larry both; I took a keen interest in their futures. Unfortunately, they never played well together. I'm not a parent, but I'm not a block of stone. Why did Larry steal from me? Good question. The boy never respected property. I should never have shown him my most prized possession, my life's work encoded. There are other ways to test loyalty. My one mistake. Larry couldn't read my code, but he was fascinated. Fifty years of true confessions, records of dark deeds. Numbers, dates, financial records. Confidential information about the greatest fortunes in the world." He held up a finger for emphasis. "One ledger of nineteen. He was going to return it to me, and I was willing to forgive and forget, but that Russian bride gambit of his was such an embarrassment. And bingo machines, what the fuck? In the end, it was prudent to jettison Larry. He was supposed to get ten years, not five. And he wasn't supposed to come back as a threat."

"And the Senator?"

Featherton's old, dead smile dropped away, revealing a toothy predator reborn. "Jimmy wouldn't give me back my ledger."

"Seems excessive," said Bob. "For a dear diary."

Featherington warmed to the subject of his ledger, assuming a geniality unwarranted by circumstance, with the nail gun pointed at his chest.

"Have you ever heard of the Voynich manuscript?"

"Of course not," said Bob.

"The rarest of all encrypted manuscripts, the Voynich manuscript surfaced in the fifteenth century and is yet to be decoded. Experts say

58

aliens wrote it."

Bob asked. "Did aliens write your book, too?"

Featherington's confident pose suggested that he expected nothing more than skepticism from Bob.

"The Feds kept their crypto techs on it for a year. They got nowhere. Nobody could crack my code. Until my boy genius, Little Jimmy Rutland found it in the evidence file. When he cracked a few pages, he called me to brag. He was going to bring it back to me, but he changed his mind. At the last minute."

Bob pointed the nail gun at the old man's face. "You don't seem to mind confessing to murder."

"Good of you to notice," said Featherington.

"This conversation may be recorded," said Bob. "Stranger things have happened."

"I never worry about that. I have an O level EMP emitter no larger than a button on my person. It isolates signature bandwidths in my voice and squelches those frequencies to white noise. Very cutting edge. I can't be recorded without my consent."

"A sound policy," said Bob. "Now get out of my shop."

"Careful with that thing," said Featherington.

Bob aimed at the old man's foot and fired a staple into his bare instep.

"Ow!" A trail of blood eked from the old man's foot. He stepped back out of his rope sandal. Bob shot him again, once above the knee and once more in his sunken ass cheek as he turned to back off. The bicycle rolled away from the door, and Bob kicked it aside. The old man ran, the bottom of his bleeding barefoot blackening instantly from the thin layer of carbon soot on the concrete floor of the parking garage. Bob kicked his sandal out of the shop and shot five staples into it.

The old man's wounds bled down his leg and left a trail as he howled with a manic edge, "You're fucked now!" His wolfish laugh echoed down the cavern of cars.

Bob shut the door to the shop and leaned back against it. The air compressor stopped chugging. In the instant of silence, Bob heard the radio call, "Fifty to Maintenance."

CHAPTER THIRTEEN
UP TO SPEED

Ed Nogg arrived in his truck, parked in his slot, and stepped out with a couple of pizzas.

Ed Nogg in a crisis stood by his man. Inside the shop, he found Bob reorganizing a forgotten cache of conduit connectors.

Ed said, "Bob, give it up. Go home."

Bob stepped down from a two-foot ladder. He asked, "What saith the King?"

Ed rolled his eyes heavenward. "David's on the fence, Bob. He doesn't want to lose you."

"I shot a guest with a nail gun," said Bob.

"Five times," said Ed.

"Three," Bob corrected. "I can easily be replaced with someone who would never do that even once."

Spots of color marked Bob's cheekbones against a waxy, gaunt pallor. Signs of stress showed in the tension of his jaw and the tight lines around his mouth.

"You shot his shoe five times," said Ed.

"His sandal," said Bob. "Just fire me, Ed. The hell with it."

"No," said Ed. "We'll get through this."

"This whole embarrassment's going to make the evening news," said Bob.

"You need to eat," said Ed. "Get your strength back. Take a pizza home. Lock the door. You're on sick leave, as of now."

"I'm scheduled to work tomorrow," said Bob.

"Negative, Ghost Rider," said Ed.

Bob switched off his radio and replaced it in its battery charger. "It's been a pleasure working with you, Ed. Sorry to cause all this shit to rain down on you."

"Don't go all gooey on me now, little buddy," said Ed. "You're not fired. You're not going to be fired."

"Don't rule it out," said Bob.

"I am ruling it out," said Ed. "Now go on. I'll clock you out on the computer. You don't have to go down to Housekeeping."

Bob opened the door. Marvin Gardener stood there, poised to knock.

"Mr. Bob Day," said Marvin, "sir, as Head of Security, it's my duty to escort you off the property."

"Whoa!" said Ed. "Bob's not fired."

Bob raised his palm to settle Ed down. "Marvin can walk me to my truck."

"You're not fired," said Ed.

Bob's black truck was backed into its regular slot twenty feet from where they stood in front of the maintenance shop doors. Marvin escorted Bob across that distance.

Marvin said, "Sorry, Bob. I do what they tell me."

Behind him, Ed stood in the doorway and shouted, "You're not fucking fired!"

"There is some doubt on that," said Marvin. "The guest wants you fired. Depending on whether he decides to press charges, you might be arrested today or tomorrow. This way, at least, you get to go home before they come for you. You don't live in Belle Rive County, do you, Bob?"

"No."

"Good, you don't want to make it easy for them. They'll have to contact your home county and secure local jurisdiction to pursue the matter. Not a done deal at all."

Bob sat behind the wheel and slowly rolled his window up on Marvin's valediction.

"Good luck to you, Bob. Come back soon."

Bob pulled out of the parking lot and turned north onto Belle Rive Boulevard, an old two-lane oceanfront road through a twelve mile stretch of prime residential real estate studded with palatial renovations, opulent new homes and stately, sturdy mansions weathering well through time and showing no outward signs of the nationwide recession.

The speed limit was a maddening twenty-five, and Belle Rive County Sheriff's deputies often backed into shaded driveways to lie in wait for speed violators. Bob took the first turn off the boulevard.

Turning north on A-1-A, he hit the gas and was soon up to speed at sixty. He had his cell phone in hand dialing Berne Ventine's secure line when he felt it vibrate with another call. He answered it out of reflex.

"Hello."

Shania Doyle said, "The biggest story in Lodge history and you didn't call me?"

"I can't talk to you," said Bob.

"Well, you better," she said.

He hung up without answering and called Berne Ventine.

"Hello, Bob." Berne's voice resonated with concern. "Having another rough day?"

"Berne, that old man knows everything about me. He mentioned my grandson. How does he know about me? You need to check on Eliza and Tim."

"Done," said Berne. "You got enough blood pressure meds?"

"Did you ever get around to bugging the shop?" Bob waited for an answer.

"No, we wouldn't do that. I was kidding when I said we would. You can't take a joke?"

"Evidently not, but if you did bug the shop, you'd have Featherington's confession, only it would sound like white noise because of his EMP emitter."

"There's no such thing as an EMP emitter," said Berne.

"You wouldn't say that if you had one," said Bob.

"Bob, you are due for a dose of tough love," said Berne.

"So are you," said Bob. "The black book is Featherington's ledger."

"Featherington's an alias," said Berne. "Featherton, Raleigh P. runs a traveling carnival."

"Featherton, then," said Bob. "Is he the Mr. Big you're after?"

"There is no Mr. Big in the Dixie Mafia," said Berne. "The DM's not structured like that. But in money laundering circles, as I'm told by those who know, no one's bigger than Uncle Raleigh."

"So, if I get arrested today or tomorrow," said Bob, "for assaulting him with a deadly weapon, you can still make it all go away, right?"

Ed answered slyly, "Depends. What's on the horizon?"

"Berne," said Bob, "you were right. I'm no Josey Wales."

"No, I was wrong," said Berne. "You are him."

"If it had been a firearm in my hand today, Featherington would have called my bluff," said Bob. "I wouldn't have had it in me to pull the trigger."

"If you had shot and killed him inside the shop, we could have written it off as self-defense, but you had to run him down and maim him."

"Have your fun," said Bob. "Just get me out of here."

"Live by the nail gun, die by the nail gun," said Berne.

Bob pulled into the parking lot of his apartment complex and rolled slowly over a series of speed bumps. He parked in his space and looked around. Some Mexicans were cooking on a hibachi grill set up on the lawn, the tiny patch of grass between the parking lot and the concrete steps. The lawn.

Bob took his pistol out of the glove box and carried it inside. He looked around his apartment for signs of trespass and saw none. He assumed his apartment had been bugged, as well as the shop, despite Berne's denials. Who was monitoring? That was the question. Some functionary, some maintenance worker with no vested interest was charged with monitoring Bob's dreary days, someone whose analysis concluded that Bob was talking to himself.

He half-filled a jelly glass with vodka and poured half the drink down his throat. He dropped into his chair and pulled off his shoes.

When the phone rang, he was down to shorts and a T-shirt and he decided not to answer it at all. But it kept ringing, so he unplugged the line.

Then his cell phone rang, and he turned it off. A little while later, there was a knock at the door. He stood to the side of his front door with his pistol cocked and loaded.

"Identify yourself," he called out.

"Detective Billy Carlisle."

"Shit," said Bob. "Have you been calling me?"

"Yes. This is an informal visit. You and I won't have this chance again."

"I'm incommunicado," Bob said.

"As well you should be, Bob," said Detective Carlisle. "I still need to ask you a few questions."

Bob slid the deadbolt back and opened the heavy metal door. "Come in," he said and quickly bolted shut the door behind Detective Carlisle.

"I have a license for this," said Bob, showing, in a non-threatening manner, his pistol to the detective.

The detective's hand moved to the pistol on his own hip.

"I'll put it up," said Bob.

Detective Carlisle stood until Bob offered him a seat at the little Formica table in the breakfast nook.

Bob poured himself another drink and waited.

Detective Carlisle eyed the drink, the bottle and Bob. He took in the steely gaze, the body language of arched shoulders and the bold forward tilt of his posture and calculated that Bob was on his third drink and that he rarely drank more than two. Not that he was drunk yet, but he was trying to get drunk.

"Bob," he asked, "Do you ever get belligerent when you drink?"

"No. Never," said Bob.

"Me either," said the detective. "See? We have that one thing in common."

"Except I'm lying," said Bob.

"Me, too," said the detective. "So where and when did you first encounter the Senator?"

"At the Lodge a few months ago. He was a guest. I unplugged his toilet."

"More recently?"

"I fixed his remote."

"And you don't follow Alabama football at all?"

Bob said, "Should I?"

The detective enunciated slowly, exaggerating the gravity of the question, "What did you talk about with the Senator yesterday afternoon besides football?"

"I have no idea," said Bob.

"He asked for you, specifically. We know that," said the detective.

"So what? I happen to be a big deal around here at the moment, or I was yesterday."

Detective Carlisle nodded, as if he had achieved a small victory.

"Saint Bob," he said. "That's what they're calling you, Saint Bob."

Bob sipped his drink. "Think I have a shot at Employee of the Month?"

Detective Carlisle made a small notation on his pad. "Funny," he said. "You think that's funny?"

"Do you?" said Bob.

"Tell me about the guest you attacked with a stapler," said the detective.

"He killed the Senator," said Bob. "It's not my job to prove it."

"Did he now," said Detective Carlisle. "Motive?"

"Ask him," said Bob.

"Bob, first of all," said Detective Carlisle, "the Senator's death, in all likelihood, was a suicide. And, second, even if it wasn't, that's how the M.E. will read it. Nobody wants a murder here. I'm just telling you how it is from my side. You can't toss around accusations."

"I can't bring you up to speed any quicker," said Bob.

"All right, Bob," said Detective Carlisle. "You're under arrest for assault."

"Really?"

"No, not really." Detective Carlisle stood and stretched his legs. "Twenty-four hours from now, who knows? That's not much of a window to straighten this out."

Bob walked him to the door. "Appreciate your concern," he said.

From the other side of the front door came a loud pounding.

"Bob! Open up! It's Shania!"

Detective Carlisle raised an eyebrow at Bob.

The pounding continued. "Let me in! Channel Twelve News is right behind me!"

Bob opened the door, and Shania rushed in. Over her shoulder, he saw the news van. He slammed the door shut.

Shania and Detective Carlisle eyed each other up and down.

"Thanks for bringing the news crew," said Bob.

"Hey, I followed them," said Shania. "Then I recognized your truck."

"I told you I'm not talking to you," said Bob.

"What about you?" she asked the detective. "You'll talk to me, won't you?"

"Absolutely," said Detective Carlisle. "Feel like a latte'?"

"Sure," said Shania. "Think I have a shot at the Mounds."

"Take those reporters with you," said Bob.

"Sorry," said Shania.

"See you tomorrow, Bob," said Detective Carlisle.

The two of them slipped out the door and into their respective vehicles. The detective followed her out past the news van as another news van pulled into the complex. The vehicles passed each other on a speed bump, the red Mazda leading the detective to Starbucks.

CHAPTER FOURTEEN
FAITH AND DOUBT

Bob disconnected his doorbell. There would be no infernal ringing.

He locked the sliding glass doors and closed the drapes and the curtains over the kitchen sink. The outer walls were concrete block and the front door was a steel sheathed solid slab of wood.

He plugged a headset into his computer speakers and fitted the earphones over his ears. He could surf the internet until he fell asleep and never hear the clamor of reporters at his door. He could ignore them and go on about his business. Except for the fact that he had no business to carry on with anywhere but in the shop.

It was the job he would miss, not the place where he lived.

Outside his apartment, the news vans were setting up for the evening news live broadcasts. Bob tuned in his television and clicked back and forth between the two local channels, both reporting on the story of the Senator's suicide. There was a shot of Bob's apartment building behind the roving reporter, Christopher Faircloth, who introduced himself and said, as he pointed to an enlarged photograph of a young Senator James T. Rutland, smiling and happy, brimming with hope, juxtaposed with a grim driver's license photo of Bob, "The medical examiner's estimated time of death suggests that there is at least a possibility that the life of the Senator from Alabama might have been saved had the Emergency Medical Technicians who were the first responders to the scene not been prevented from doing their jobs by this man, Robert Day, a maintenance worker at the Belle Rive Lodge and Club, who denied them access to the Senator's room, citing a need to 'preserve the crime scene.' Is this a case of too much CSI? Maintenance worker, Robert Day, has, so far, refused to comment."

The thrust of the other channel's story was the same. The Senator's death by suicide might have been averted had the EMTs not been denied entry by an emotionally distraught maintenance worker, who now faces possible assault charges for allegedly shooting an elderly hotel guest with a staple gun.

Bob turned up the volume.

"We go now to Merciful Skies Hospital where community correspondent, Cheryl Crenshaw, is standing by with the victim of today's staple gun attack, an eighty-two-year-old WWII veteran named Raleigh Featherington."

The featured clip showed the old man in a wheelchair with his foot bandaged in a splint. He spoke to the camera in a pitiful whine, "What kind of a hotel keeps a trigger happy animal like that on staff? He went berserk, I tell you. Like a mad dog. I lost a lot of blood."

Bob turned off the TV. He dragged himself into the bedroom and fell onto the bed. Sleep would not come. He lay for hours staring up at the ceiling, yet one look at the clock revealed that five minutes had yet to pass.

If he could not trust Berne Ventine, he could trust no one. He wasn't a hundred percent sure about Berne. There were moments when he was as sure as he could be, though, and that was the way he wished he could continue to feel about Berne, like he could trust him with his life, because he had trusted him in the past with his own life and with the lives of his family, to protect them all from harm. If that put too much pressure on Berne, maybe it was unreasonable to expect him to remain iconic, upright and incorruptible. If a U.S. Marshal could be bought, he wouldn't stay a U.S. Marshal very long. Berne had convinced Bob of that long ago. Berne had earned his trust a hundred times over. Bob felt ashamed for reserving so much judgment. Of course, he trusted Berne. He had no one else to trust.

But Berne had not confided in him. Berne had held back information. Information was not a two way street with Berne. What else had he held back?

Bob knew that Berne had to play it the U.S. Marshals way. In the past, he'd gone along with everything Berne suggested. But now the sky was falling. His world was imploding, and it was clearer than it had ever seemed before to him how dependent he was on Berne Ventine. The mask of Bob's independence was being torn away. He was not going to be able to continue for much longer as Bob Day of the Lodge and Club. Without that identity, he would become a blank slate again. He felt like a little *Claymation* figure singing a jingle in a toy commercial, "Bend me, shape me, any way you want me. Long as you love me, it's all right."

He was Bob Clay, saying to Berne, in so many words, "Do with me what you will."

He had no problem giving Berne the benefit of the doubt. It was having the doubt in the first place that was the problem, and never having a sense of perfect trust, like when you fall back knowing someone will catch you. Never doubting, never having doubt; to have faith in, to believe. Bob's trust issues did not allow him to believe that blindly anymore.

Always there was doubt, and doubt was poison.

The sole antidote was faith. If Bob chose to believe in Berne, to take his word, to believe that Berne Ventine would not lie to him, the choice would neutralize the doubt. He would still be completely dependent on Berne, but he would not mind it as much.

Bob turned the TV back on. Action News was rerunning the clip where the old man had called him trigger happy. Past the point where Bob had turned it off, the clip continued. The old man coughed into his hand, looked at his palm and coughed again. Then his face cracked wide in a wincing grimace of pain, and his left arm curled close across his chest like a withering vine. He leaned over the side of his wheelchair and tipped it over. The camera followed him to the ground where he writhed for a moment before he died; a live action heart attack.

After a moment of stupefaction, Bob plugged in the phone and called the shop.

Ed picked up. "Hey, Bob. How are you holding up?"

"I've had better days."

"I take it you've seen the news?"

"Just now. Have you?"

"No, but I've got three emails so far from across the street, telling me about it."

"Am I fired yet?"

"No, but don't kill anybody else."

"Et tu?" said Bob.

Ed laughed long and loud, striking a note of earnest bravado that rang true, false, and true again too quickly for Bob to discern the changes.

"I tried to call you awhile ago," Ed said, "to remind you about the employee rally tomorrow."

"Tomorrow's Sunday."

"I mean Monday. O ten hundred hours. The Palm Room. No, wait, the Ocean Room."

"I might not make it," said Bob.

"Oh, you'll make it," said Ed.

"If I'm not arrested by then," said Bob.

"If you're not arrested by then, you probably won't be," said Ed.

"That's a big if," said Bob.

CHAPTER FIFTEEN
SUNDAY EDITION

Early Sunday morning Bob went out to buy a paper. The TV news vans were gone. He took his bicycle for a ride and brought back the Sunday edition of the Florida Times-Union.

There was a story in the Metro section about Senator Rutland from Alabama, discovered dead Saturday morning in his hotel suite at the Lodge by a maintenance man. Written by Shania Doyle, the story touched all the salient points, including the anecdotal saga of Raleigh Featherington, the elderly hotel guest allegedly assaulted with a staple gun, whose death later that day from a heart attack during a live TV news broadcast was allegedly not unrelated to his staple wounds.

One could argue that Featherington's heart attack was not unrelated to his age, either, or to his medical condition prior to the staple wounds, but Bob was not arguing. The death clip video was already an internet sensation, garnering tens of thousands of hits from around the globe on YouTube.

Bob skimmed the article, then went back and read it again.

Was the Senator's death an assisted suicide? That was one question Shania raised that remained unanswered. Detective William Carlisle had offered no official opinion, yea or nay. His inclination not to rule out homicide had yet to be superseded or confirmed by physical evidence.

"So much depends upon the medical examiner's report," Detective Carlisle was quoted as saying. "However much we all might like to follow hunches sometimes, in the end, we are guided by the facts."

As he read, Bob frowned and muttered, "How poetic."

The facts in Shania's timeline were: Thursday morning around nine o'clock, Senator Rutland kissed his wife goodbye in Birmingham, Alabama and drove his own car alone straight through to Belle Rive County, Florida, where he claimed his reservation and checked into the Lodge around four o'clock.

Three hours later, at seven o'clock, Raleigh Featherington checked into his room two doors down from the Senator.

On Friday, the Senator hardly left his suite. He ordered room service and enjoyed his privacy. He was seen that afternoon on his patio balcony, reading and relaxing alone. If he had any visitors, they came and went unobserved. Room Service, Housekeeping and Maintenance staff all had access to his room. Of these departments, maintenance worker, Robert Day, the last known person to see the Senator alive, is confirmed to have spent at least a half an hour that Friday afternoon with the Senator, allegedly discussing football.

Robert Day finished his shift and clocked out at four o'clock.

Around seven o'clock, Friday evening, the Senator called Housekeeping to waive turndown service and request extra towels. Towels were delivered and left outside the door, as per his request.

Saturday morning, a little before ten, Robert Day discovered Senator Rutland's lifeless body in the bathtub of his suite with both wrists cut and the tub filled with blood and water. Day used his radio to notify the front desk manager on duty, Constance Featherton, to call 911. At that time, he observed drip stains on the walls and ceiling that appeared to be splash marks made with bloody water, and yet, the bathroom floor was completely dry, as if it had been wiped.

Based on the floor being dry, Day made the determination that the Senator's apparent suicide may not have been unassisted. In an effort to preserve the integrity of the "crime scene," Day denied access to the first responders, the Emergency Medical Technicians, prior to the arrival of law enforcement personnel.

Detective William Carlisle arrived on the scene and confirmed Day's observation that the bathroom floor appeared to have been wiped dry. The detective refused to speculate whether the so-called 'suicide' may have involved another person.

Preliminary findings of the medical examiner estimated the time of death on Saturday morning, between five-thirty and nine-thirty. Bob recognized that the unfortunate timing indicated that the Senator, if he was indeed dead at the time of his discovery, had not been dead long when Bob prevented the EMTs from entering his suite.

Shania's efforts to be evenhanded in her treatment of Robert Day's descent into the swirling suction of bad press failed to de-emphasize the depth of the grave he had dug for himself by being helpful. Bob's good intentions were easily overshadowed by the perception of his reckless lapse of judgment.

The concurrent story of Raleigh Featherington continued where the Senator's ended.

Raleigh Featherington turned out to be an alias of the illustrious Raleigh Featherton, past President of the Showmen's League of America, and owner of East-West Entertainment Group, parent company of one of the last and largest traveling carnivals in the country.

Bob put down the paper and wondered why he had not been arrested. Having been named as a "person of interest" in two deaths occurring on the same day, it was inevitable, he thought; the gendarmes would soon have him sweating under hot lights in a windowless room, chained to a sturdy table where other hardened criminals had wept, confessed, and begged for mercy.

And where was Constance in Shania's story? Had she overlooked the possible involvement of Raleigh Featherton's grand niece? Apparently so, as no mention was made in her article of family ties.

Constance would have facilitated her great uncle's accommodations, since that was exactly her job. And the timing of his arrival, three hours after the Senator, how fortuitous! Conclusion: Constance and Raleigh Featherton were not as distant as she claimed.

Constance. The very thought of her made his palm ache for a weapon. Not that he would have ever succumbed to the urge to use it on her, but her insipid yet condescending smile served to focus his resolve.

Bob gathered his kit and headed out.

The shooting range was crowded for a Sunday morning. The first car Bob recognized in the lot was Shania's red Mazda. As his heartbeat quickened, he exhaled fully, emptying his lungs. Inhaling through his nose in short bursts, he gathered in ki. He'd seen the breathing technique in a Bruce Lee movie calm Bruce down. It didn't seem to work as well for Bob, although maybe he wasn't doing it right. He soldiered on, parked the truck and went inside, knowing he would see Shania and that, between them, obligatory niceties would be exchanged.

All the things that he had come to the shooting range to escape from were waiting for him there at the shooting range.

And more, much more than this; there was a man with his arms around Shania.

Detective Billy Carlisle was embracing her. She was leaning into him like a lover, acting girlish with Billy. He was giving her shooting tips, and she was pretending to be impressed with his swaggering manliness.

Something fell off inside Bob, some integral piece of his inner structure weakened and snapped like a sheared piece of metal, like a cotter pin failing and falling out of its critical slot. He could almost hear the metallic ping it would have made dropping onto a concrete floor, instead of its soundless disappearance into the carpeted floor of his mind. The cotter pin broke and things kept tightly wrapped began to unravel. Things started spilling out.

Deep inside the deepest part of him he felt the loss of that cotter pin. Habit held his spirit together, kept things in proper sequence and not flooding out in all directions like a chaotic stream. That was not Bob, emotionally crippled, or hobbled with age. Or was it? What it all meant to Bob in that moment of seeing Shania melting into Billy Carlisle's broad chest was the gut realization, without sugarcoating anything, that it was all over for him at that point. Everything that mattered was over and done with.

"Never mind," he chided himself. "You're sixty-one. Act your age."

Bob adjusted his ear protection and started shooting. In the back of his mind, he kept thinking, "Hannie Caulder is no more."

Billy separated himself from Shania and came over to say hello.

"Hey, Bob," he said when Bob finished a round.

"Detective," said Bob.

Bob loaded another magazine and prepared to shoot again.

Billy stood by waiting for Bob to respond to his overture, to see that he was being friendly and engage with him in a dialogue. His patience began to evaporate as he saw that wasn't about to happen.

"How we doing, Bob?"

"You got a mouse in your pocket?"

Billy chuckled a shade too heartily at that old joke. "So what's going on, Bob?"

"You tell me," said Bob.

"I think I know what's going on," said Billy. "You can tell me if I'm correct."

Bob said, "I am not having that conversation."

"Bob, it's not like that," said Billy. "I'm not looking to take you in."

"I'm not obliged to talk to anyone," said Bob.

"I can understand that," said Billy. "And I think it's wise that you draw the line across the board. I mean, don't trust me. Don't trust anybody."

Bob said, "I've got nothing else to say to you."

"Well, all right," said Billy. "Till you feel otherwise. I won't keep you. Shania wants to talk to you, too, Bob. You know, it's in your best interests to talk to us, to both of us."

"I don't want to talk to either one of you, alone or separately," said Bob. "What are you going to tell me, anyway? Never mind what I can tell you, what can you tell me? Can you tell me when I'm going to be arrested? Will you tell me any information at all about my case? No. You just want me to tell you things."

"Simmer down, Bob," said Billy.

Bob seethed with wounded dignity, his blood pressure spiking. At such times his face and scalp reddened and the flushed feeling would leave him dizzy after a few minutes of hypertension. What used to be called "seeing red" described it well enough but the red was transitory. When it passed, it was over. The intensity faded, leaving behind a loss of passion. So grows apathy, as memories fade.

Bob aimed his pistol again and shot six more rounds. He let the weight of it hang at the end of his arm. He breathed deeply, and his heart rate calmed as Billy Carlisle left. Billy said something to Shania on his way out. Bob reached for the comet trail of his old serenity. He would bounce back. But he would never bounce all the way back again. He'd just be going through the motions. That was the realization of his day: that he was done.

There was a measure of serenity in that, and Bob had regained some of it when Shania came up to him. Until then, he was fine, aiming at targets and shooting them, practicing, aiming, developing the skills of his hobby. The single-minded clarity of the shot being fired shut out everything unrelated. He was able to lose himself and let that singular focus take over. It was a comfort to him to understand such things, especially when they couldn't be explained.

He saw Shania walking towards him without moving his head to look at her. His peripheral vision was fair to middling. Before he saw her, he felt her eyes on him. He sensed her, half-skipping toward him, a lilt in her step.

"Hey, Bob," she said, with concern in her voice.

"Hey, yourself. Yes, I did read your article. It was a very good article, and you couldn't have been fairer to me. Congratulations on a great career that you might have ahead of you because, yes, it could have been a lot worse."

"It could have been a lot worse," she admitted.

"Yes, it could have been a lot worse."

"I didn't want to hurt you, Bob. I didn't try to hurt you. Bob, I think you might be right. I actually believe you, Bob. I think you might be right about Featherton. I really would like to talk to you about that."

"I'm not going to talk about it," said Bob.

"Bob," she said, "I believe you. I believe you. I. Believe. You."

"You don't believe me," said Bob.

"I do. I do believe you. I've talked to Billy, and I know what he said, and I know what he thinks. Billy believes you, too, but he can't come out and support you. That's just not possible, Bob, until we can prove something."

"There's no proving anything because Raleigh Featherton is dead."

"Yeah," she said, "isn't that weird?"

"Quite weird," said Bob.

"Well, all I know is, he was a lot healthier going into that hospital than he was when he came out of it."

Bob looked up and caught the inquisitive spark in her eye.

"What does that tell you?" he asked.

"He walked into the hospital. And the wounds themselves, well, Bob; you know where you shot him. Those were not fatal wounds."

"I didn't think they were," said Bob.

"No, they were not fatal wounds," she said. "And yet, he had a heart attack. Sure, but did you hear what he said? 'I lost a lot of blood,' How much blood do you lose from a staple shot? I mean, really. Did it hit an artery? No. Is he a hemophiliac? No."

"If he was on Coumadin, he might have been a bleeder," said Bob. "But he was in the hospital. They would have known."

"I know. That's what I'm saying. He came out worse than he went in."

"Shania, I am not submitting to any more interviews. There is no way I'm going to collaborate with you on your next story."

76

She leaned up and kissed him on the cheek. That sealed her in glory forever, before she had said a word. It wasn't like he was hard to reach. If anything, he was way too easy.

She said, "Take care, Bob. Call me when you feel like talking, or I'll call you if you don't call me. I know where you live. I'll come by. That's just the way I am. Oh, you don't like seeing me hanging out with Billy. Don't worry, Bob, I'm on top of this. It's okay, Bob, you're still Bob Culp to me, Bob."

That reached him. He couldn't help it. She was after his heart. Bob watched her walk away, in her thrall again.

CHAPTER SIXTEEN
EMPLOYEE RALLY

Back in the shop on Monday, Bob put on a pot of his fiercest motivational blend. He rarely drank a second cup, so his one cup in the morning had to be stronger than strong. It was hard on all day coffee drinkers like Karl, who would drink four or five cups a day of most any coffee except Bob's. A second cup of Bob's famous java and Karl was liable to abandon his reserve and start pontificating on world politics or celebrity gossip.

Karl had not been around all weekend, but surely he had heard or seen some news of the situation. Bob heard Karl's old Volvo wheeze into a parking slot outside the shop. He heard his footsteps approach.

Karl entered with a stifled yawn. The tableau he encountered every day upon opening the door could have been a Norman Rockwell scene: a subterranean workshop with tools hanging from corkboards and crowded shelves packed with supplies and workbenches cluttered with unopened packages. A utilitarian organization of every inch of available space added a perception of depth. In all the shop, there was one blank shelf, which, for his sanity's sake, Bob kept inviolate with a hand-lettered cardboard sign that read: This Item Sold Out.

Bob, in his customary spot near the door, stood with his left leg propped on the air compressor, a Styrofoam cup of black mud in his hand.

"Morning, Bob," said Karl.

"Morning, Karl."

Karl went straight to the coffee pot, filled a cup, moved to the workbench and set his coffee down on the belt sander.

"Well, Bob," said Karl, "ask me about my weekend."

Bob raised an eyebrow and asked, "Did you take the family to Stone Mountain as planned?"

"No. We were delayed at the Vidalia Onion Festival. One of The Seven Wonders of Georgia."

"And a good time was had by all," said Bob.

"Yeah," said Karl. "Top that."

Karl kept a straight face, as did Bob. As soon as Bob cracked a smile, Karl's mission was accomplished. For Karl, every day was Make Bob Laugh Day. If he could make Bob laugh in the morning, before Ed or anyone else arrived, that was the best part of his work day. The rest of the day he could keep himself amused.

Too soon, others in the crew would arrive and the make Bob laugh part of Karl's day would end. Maybe later Karl would get another chance to make Bob laugh. For the moment, they were both laughing. Bob had not laughed much the last couple of days.

If Karl had not read about or heard what had transpired over the weekend at the Lodge while he was off at the Vidalia Onion Festival, then what was he laughing at, Bob wondered. What was so funny? Not that it mattered. It was a relief, in any case, that Karl saw fit to ask no questions, like it was just another day in paradise.

• • • • •

The motivational speaker booked for that day's Employee Rally arrived in a black stretch limo along with his entourage. Four suites had been reserved for his party. At the front desk, he booked four more rooms.

The speaker that day had a whirlwind career going. He'd written a few motivational books and handed them out like party favors at every whistle stop on his speaking tour, slim volumes with titles like *Ten Steps to Financial Freedom* and *Bus Driver*.

The Lodge employees herded themselves into the Ocean Room, the largest of the meeting rooms. Refreshment tables lined the outer wall of windows overlooking the ocean from the second floor. Scones, bagels, cookies, croissants, orange juice and coffee. At least once a year, employees were rewarded with a light brunch of sweetmeats and a motivational speaker to spur them on to ever greater heights of dedication.

Chef BooHoo from the Oasis kitchen, so nicknamed for his Mike Tyson on helium voice, filed in with Vlad. They took seats in the front right corner behind Shadowlip, Miss Intensity, Chef Skank and the Ferret. One by one, they all noticed or pretended not to notice Bob in his seat in the back row on the left with Ed and Karl and the rest of the maintenance staff, Gene and Dustin.

Irina entered with Mikhail. They were an odd sight, walking and talking together, the Czech housekeeper and the Bosnian bellman.

Mikhail took a seat behind Vlad, spoke a word into his ear, and Vlad got up and moved back a row beside Irina.

The Lodge's own Training Coordinator, John Thomas, introduced the speaker. There was a time when employee orientation at the Lodge was a thriving department in and of itself, a time when John Thomas led a different class of new hires through a tour of the property twice a month, and every ninety days offered a refresher course in the five-diamond level of hotel service.

There hadn't been regular new hire orientations at the Lodge for quite some time. The employees that remained were mostly long term survivors. So John Thomas sponsoring a rally with a professional motivational speaker seemed curiously ill-timed and gave all employees pause to wonder what kind of budget a one-man department like his must have to be throwing that kind of money around when every other department was cut to the bone. By some angelic fiat, John Thomas still had his job motivating people to work harder, smile more, and believe, above all, that they "are the best in the world at what they do."

John Thomas incorporated music into his slideshow presentation.

He'd throw in snippets of familiar songs to get your attention, to present himself as a fun loving, happy family gathering sort of guy, lip singing along with hip dance moves, *"What they do? They smile in your face ..."*

Maybe he did cut up a little too much at the last supervisors' summit and maybe his reputation as a drunk was deserved. Maybe he would be better off if he didn't drink at all, but he was just having fun, testing the limits. He could still be trusted to represent the corporate line. And if there was a song you liked in his slideshow, you were more inclined to trust him than not.

When the music stopped, John Thomas would exhort his captive audiences to renew their dedication to the virtues of attitude, enthusiasm and inspiration. He was in the business of exuding enthusiasm at all times, even in the most challenging situations, such as when introducing a fellow professional who had taken the craft of motivational speaking beyond the local level.

That wasn't fair, they were on different paths. John Thomas harbored no jealousy.

"And so, ladies and gentlemen," said John Thomas, "without further ado, our guest speaker, Art Chase."

In his early thirties, Art Chase had formerly worked as a waiter at the Lodge, so his return nine years later was a homecoming for him, although no one remembered his employment stint and none of his former colleagues remained on staff.

No stranger to adversity, Art Chase had failed life's every challenge, by his own admission, until about two and a half years ago. He'd lost his job and could find no other. His marriage crumbled. He'd run through his savings, borrowed from his parents and maxed out his credit cards. In his darkest hour, he decided to reinvent himself as a motivational speaker.

He wrote *Bus Driver*, which posed the motivational question, "Are you going to ride the bus or are you going to drive the bus?" The book struck a nerve with readers and amped his confidence enough for him to speak at a conference of self-help book authors.

To his chagrin as he got up to the podium to speak at the conference, he spotted in the front row the great granddaddy lion of all motivational speakers, Zig Ziglar. After he spoke, Zig Ziglar shook his hand and told him to keep at it. Art Chase had never looked back and now look at him: in demand at employee rallies all over the country. And it all had started with the one little question, "Are you going to drive the bus or ride the bus?"

"If you're not driving the bus," Art Chase said, "you need to know who is driving the bus and you need to know where that bus is going, don't you?"

Edelberto, the houseman, said something in Tagalog and all the Filipinos chuckled.

Karl reached over the seat and tapped the houseman, Rey, on the shoulder. Rey looked back and translated, "Edelberto say he drive elevator."

Karl repeated to Bob, "Edelberto said he drives the elevator."

Ed Nogg repeated the line to Gene on his right, who repeated it to Dustin.

Bob was sitting between Ed and Karl until Karl responded to a tap on his own shoulder. He got up and moved, and David Moriarty slid into the vacated chair to Bob's left.

"Hey, Bob, how are you doing?" said David, offering his hand.

Bob shook David Moriarty's hand. "As well as can be expected," he said.

"Welcome back," said David.

"Thanks."

As General Manager of the Lodge and Club, David Moriarty oversaw all operations and kept a responsible eye on the bottom line, which was why the Lodge was still in the black in this leanest of lean years. An accountant first, he had to answer to the owners when they asked the big questions. Neither of them wanted to hear about the dire condition of the roof, which would cost almost a million dollars to replace. The building was less than thirty years old, but it had been built on a sand dune during the height of the red hot construction boom in North Florida. Oceanfront building codes had evolved since the mid nineteen eighties.

The building was riddled with structural problems. The stucco exterior had weathered well against the ocean winds and rain. The tile roof had not held up. The underlayment had failed in too many places. Plywood rotting under the tiles was especially visible in sections under the eaves. During a heavy rain, twenty buckets were strategically placed on the Ocean Room floor to catch drips from the ceiling. But it was true, as optimists said, that most of the time, the roof was fine, except when it rained. Everyone knew the Lodge needed a new roof, but roof repair was not even on the back burner at the Owners Meetings.

Other priorities took precedence, like the possible sale of the minority shares in the Lodge. David Moriarty was privy to the knowledge that the idea of the sale had been floated at the last Owners Meeting. Those shares, he believed, would be offered to him, at the next Owners Meeting, if there was any justice, in recognition of his stewardship.

David had cut the budget to the bone already. Old standbys like the Employee Christmas Party and free employee lunches had already been canceled. Staff cuts in every department had winnowed down the hotel payroll, yet the Lodge continued to retain its four-diamond standard rating, thanks in no small part to David's keen eye for aesthetics.

The coveted five-diamond rating continued to elude the Lodge and Club. Yet David saw to it that the Lodge never stopped striving for it.

The onus was on David Moriarty to steer the narrow line between keeping up appearances and fiscal responsibility. General Manager of the Lodge and Club was a high-stress position. And there was no one close to him in whom he could confide. His was a solitary burden. And sometimes he felt like laying it down. But it was never his way to give up. It had been a very long time since David Moriarty had given up at anything. He trained for the triathlon every year and had competed with distinction the last five years. He was fit under his suit. He had stamina and endurance. He was in it for the long haul.

David watched Art Chase's presentation with a pen in hand and took notes. Bob couldn't read them and didn't try, but he watched the King, peripherally, jot and scribble on a pad like a dedicated student.

Art Chase told a few jokes, a few anecdotes. Then he asked a rhetorical multiple choice question and David leaned toward Bob and confided, "I'm going with C. It's always C."

The realization that David Moriarty was privately kidding around with him made Bob wonder what might happen next. David leaned in again to ask Bob, in a low voice that was more than a whisper, "Bob, if I may, I'd like to ask you one question, not a multiple choice."

"Shoot," said Bob.

"Um, what were you thinking when you shot a guest with a nail gun?"

"I wouldn't call it thinking," said Bob.

David winced as if that were not the best answer he could have hoped for.

"Before I go," said Art Chase, "It's my honor to introduce a fellow motivational speaker who has been a tremendous inspiration to me." He smiled at John Thomas and continued, "But first, I want to thank John Thomas for bringing me in to be part of his show."

Mild applause followed, and the shadow of uncertainty flickered on John Thomas' face, reflecting an instant of doubt before he shook it off with a professional smile and shook Art Chase's hand.

Art kept the mike and announced, "My special guest today is my new publisher, Lee J. Wilkes of Red Door Books. You want inspiration? Here's a guy who came to America a penniless immigrant with nothing but the clothes on his back. He spoke no English, had no trade. But he was young and strong and he found work. He dug ditches, washed dishes, learned English, learned to drive trucks, became a citizen, built a business of his own and thrived in America because he was willing to work hard. No other reason. There is no other key to success but hard work. At least, that's what I hear. And I'm pretty sure it's true. So, here to add a few words on the topic of success is the founder and publisher of Red Door Books, my good friend, Mr. Lee J. Wilkes."

The gentleman who stepped onto the dais in a casual yet distinguished Armani suit was tall with a sculpted silver beard and the sharp profile of a falcon. He looked like new money, almost like old money, but not quite.

As his piercing gray eyes swept over the small audience, Bob recognized him. It had been over four years, but those eyes still commanded attention. Lee J. Wilkes, like Larry "the Cherry" Wilhoite, was one more alias of Aronoyad Wilgushku.

Lee J. Wilkes beamed magisterially at the employees. "Thanking you peoples for having me," he said, his accent a lingering trace of old country origins and an amalgam of affectations.

"When I was a young man, I knew everything. My father told me I was a fool. Did I believe him? No. Was he right? Yes. In my country, fathers are always right. Ask any father. I was a fool, and my father was right. Those two things could never change. I felt this. But I was a fool, so what did I know? Nothing. What did I feel? Everything.

"When you are young, you feel. You call it thinking, but it is feeling. All your decisions are based on feeling. Everything you do when you are young, you do because you feel. Later, you think more and feel less. You are never the same after that, once you lost that loving feeling, when everything, everything is about how it feels."

Ed Nogg leaned toward Bob and said, "What in the fuck is he talking about?"

Bob stared straight ahead with no expression. The upward lift in the corners of his tightened lips was due to the clenching of his jaw.

David spoke in a low voice into his other ear, "I have to have some kind of explanation why I don't fire you."

Lee J. Wilkes looked out over the heads of his audience, through the window walls to the sea beyond, his vision so much larger than the room.

"Thinking and feeling are two different ways," he said, "but they can lead to the same place. Like being old and being young can merge. I would ask those of you who are older to remember the times when your feelings were so strong that you could not think, you could only feel. And those of you who are younger, I ask you to think while you can still feel everything, so you will never forget the difference. When you follow your heart's desire, that is feeling. When you do what you have to do, that is thinking. Between the two lies the balance of emotional health that leads to success."

David Moriarty continued to whisper to Bob, "For example, if your answer is 'I have a problem,' be it anger management, substance abuse or alcohol, the company will pay for rehab and there's no question of losing your job. But if rehab's not the issue, what is? Impulse control? They don't have rehab for that. I don't think. You see what I'm saying?"

"I think so," said Bob. "I mean, I feel as if I do."

Lee J. Wilkes bowed at the close of his little speech and basked in the sporadic applause. He looked out over the faces in the assembly and the maintenance men in the back row. His eye settled on Bob.

Eye contact between the two held secrets. Long seconds passed. Bob processed the Lee J. Wilkes identity: Publishing books was a step up from publishing a Russian bride directory. That periodical, distributed at bus stops and laundromats, was put out by an outfit called Green Door Publishing. Green Door Publishing doing business as Red Door Books was not a giant leap. But the persona of Lee J. Wilkes, Publisher, that feat had required planning, and organization.

Bob refused to look away. Lee J. Wilkes bowed again with a nod to Bob and left the rally room with Art Chase. The rally wrapped up with a nod from John Thomas and the employees were released, to linger and mingle over croissants, coffee, juice and scones.

As the maintenance crew began to wander back toward the shop from the Ocean Room, Ed Nogg said, "Bob, you know that guy?"

"No," said Bob.

"You sure? It looked like he recognized you. He didn't look at anybody else."

"He was probably imagining me naked," said Bob. "That old Toastmasters trick."

CHAPTER SEVENTEEN
RED DOOR

A second rally at two o'clock was scheduled for all staff members who could not attend the first show. Lee J. Wilkes was not expected to appear.

Irina had brought him extra towels. She left the room with color rising in her throat and cheeks as he blew her a little kiss.

Lee J. Wilkes was settled in the Presidential Suite. He had a meeting scheduled later with the Membership Director, Diana Bytheway.

His plan resembled a line of dominoes poised to fall in succession. Once he charmed Ms. Bytheway and gained her support, he would buy into the Lodge, become a member and bring in a few trusted friends as guests, implement their provisional memberships and form the nucleus of a power base, take the helm, take over, turn the place around; make it hot and stylish, hot, young and stylish. Not so full of old folks.

The Lodge was like a castle by the sea. Castlemare was a more romantic name. There would be a lot of big changes for the Lodge, for Castlemare, in his plan.

The members of his entourage were all without exceptions sons and daughters of America's wealthiest elite, profligate scions of heirs and heiresses to enormous fortunes, the glitterati. All had ended up in chronic rehab treatment centers, their lives proven time and again to be unmanageable due to their addictions.

Drugs, alcohol, gambling, sex; whatever substance or act held sway over a prospect mattered not at all to Wilkes because he wielded greater power. Addictions mysteriously paled away under his tutelage. He offered something more.

Wilkes stood on the patio watching the ocean with a cell phone held to his ear, the white terrycloth robe cinched snug around his lean waist. His laugh was full of affection for an old friend. "Marconi, no," he said, "Marconi, listen to me, compadre, if I never sell another Russian bride it is okay for me. This is so much better. This is the best one of all, Marconi, no, the best."

He stopped talking for a moment to watch a dark-haired jogger run past. "Excuse me, a stunning woman." He leaned over the balcony to view Claudia's perfect glutes in liquid motion.

"Goodness. Yes, Red Door Enterprises. Red Door Talent and Entertainment Agency. I tell them peoples I represent all talent, entertainment: photography, film, music, art, dance, circus, everything under the sun. Red Door Productions, Red Door Films. Red Door Books. World rights video usage fees in every contract. DVD, Blu-Ray."

Wilkes leaned on his balcony railing overlooking the beach and watched Claudia jog into the distance.

"Yes, Mr. Blofeld, sir, I say, yes, you have my golden word, your son or daughter will be gainfully employed in motion picture industry as soon as he or she completes the training course at Red Door Institute, where health and safety of our charges at all times is first concern of Red Door Security Systems, twenty-four seven. My full assurance in the matter, yes."

He chuckled into the phone, "Marconi, listen to me, listen. They are so beautiful, these peoples, and they know how the money moves already. It is second nature for them to be actors, spies and thieves."

He laughed at something Marconi said. "Yes, I am miracle worker. Yes, I am. Ha-ha. Goodbye, Marconi."

Wilkes dropped his hearty smile as he dropped the phone into the pocket of his robe. Marconi was an old friend, but there was no need to confide in him like that. Now he would have to kill him. Ha, not really. Not yet.

He dialed the front desk and asked to speak to Constance. When she came to the phone his voice took on a reverent tone. "Hello, my love, my sweet, Connie. Once again I have returned to service you with my enormous manhood."

Constance hung up, and Wilkes' hollow chuckle sounded unconvincing even to his own ears. He looked out to sea and whispered, "You love it."

Wilkes came inside and shut the patio door.

In the sudden absence of the ocean's rhythm, he heard a knock and a voice from outside announce, "Maintenance."

He opened the front door, and the maintenance man was there. His name tag read BOB.

Wilkes stepped back and said, "Please come in, Mr. Deighton."

"The name is Day," said Bob. "Bob Day."

"As you say," said Wilkes. "Mr. Day, tell me all your troubles."

"My concern," said Bob, "is that you may think, or feel, that you and I have unfinished business."

Wilkes dismissed the notion. "And why under heaven of God would I think such thing?"

"I know of no sane reason," said Bob.

"Do you say I am insane?"

"No, but if that is accurate information, it behooves me to know," said Bob.

"It is very inaccurate information. I should seek revenge on you for doing your civic duty in America? Risk my God-given parole for you? No, Mr. Day. I am so over you, as children say."

Wilkes snapped his fingers twice in front of Bob's face. "You are so four years ago. Ha. What a disguise, by the way. Hide in plain sight. Will they allow you to keep your uniforms after you are fired?"

"That's up in the air," said Bob.

"I hope for your sake, yes, but no, between us there is no bone to pick as regards my four long years in federal hellhole prison. But I also have questions."

Bob said, "What kind of parole lets you leave the state?"

"The kind I have," said Lee J. Wilkes.

"What about the threats you made."

"I renounce them. I retract them all."

"Why did you come here, then?"

"My turn," said Lee J. Wilkes, "one question."

"You knew the Senator had the book," said Bob.

"What book," said Wilkes.

"Please," said Bob, "that's your question?"

"Where is book?" Wilkes asked.

"Who knows? Who cares? Only you," said Bob. "Why? You can't read it."

Wilkes smiled like the flashing of a blade.

"Uncle Raleigh told you that. A little knowledge is a dangerous thing."

"Why are you here?" said Bob.

Wilkes moved toward the door. He said, "We have closure now, yes?"

Wilkes opened the door and held it for Bob.

Bob said, "You call this closure?"

Wilkes' indifferent countenance gave nothing away.

Bob left the room, and the door closed behind him.

Wilkes returned to the balcony to gaze out at the tranquil sea.

"My thoughts be not so bloody anymore," he spoke to the calming sea and sky.

CHAPTER EIGHTEEN
CONCORDANCE

Bob walked away from the Presidential suite with a feeling that he had been lied to by the Prince of Liars.

"Fifty to Maintenance."

Bob unclipped the radio from his belt and answered, "Go ahead, Fifty."

"Will you check the temperature here behind the front desk, please? It's very stuffy, and the thermostat doesn't seem to be working."

The air handler responsible for the front desk area operated in tandem with the one for the lobby, which was always overworked due to the large amount of open space it regulated. In summer, too hot, in winter, too cold; in spring and fall it could be either, several times a day.

A request to raise or lower the temperature by a degree or two in the front desk area was usually treated as a minor inconvenience, but Bob felt a little less cantankerous since his return to work, and if eternal vigilance was to be the price of keeping his job, so be it.

A little heart to heart with Constance, however futile, was overdue.

"The thermostat is fine, Bob," said Constance when he appeared before her. "I just would like a word with you."

She met him at her door and invited him into her office. On the wall next to the light switch was a smudged chip in the paint where the flyspeck had been removed. The tiny arrow and his name were covered now by a decal of the Lodge logo, a sea shell.

Constance closed the door behind him. "Please, have a seat, Bob," she said.

Bob remained standing with his hand on the other chair until she settled into her own desk chair. Then he sat.

"To what do I owe the honor?" said Bob.

"Bob," said Constance, "I know you didn't kill my Grand Uncle Raleigh."

90

Bob found himself agreeing with her for the first time.

"How can you be so sure?"

Constance shook her head. "You're in way over your head, Bob. You don't know who you're dealing with."

"Enlighten me," said Bob.

"Can you stop being smug for one second, please? What I'm trying to tell you might save your life."

Bob said, "I'm sorry, what?" The new, helpful version of Constance was disconcerting.

"We are all in danger here," said Constance. "The Lodge is in danger. You don't know these people."

"Do you?"

"As a matter of fact, I do." Constance let the plastic glaze fall away from her face like a mask dropping. "My family has a history, Bob. I've been around gypsies and travelers and carny people all my life. Well, not all. I got away."

"Your Uncle Raleigh was king of the carnies, wasn't he?"

"Until he was killed."

"Sorry about that," said Bob.

"It happened in the hospital. You didn't do it," she said.

"Was he on Coumadin?"

"What?"

"Coumadin. Blood thinner. Had he ever had a stroke previously?"

"Yes. Maybe. Probably. I don't know," said Constance.

"If he was on Coumadin, I probably did kill him. Even though his wounds were bandaged, he could have kept losing blood internally."

"He had a massive heart attack," said Constance.

"I saw the clip," said Bob.

"That was not from bleeding."

"From what, then?"

"I don't know, but Mikhail was there at the hospital. He's Ari's cousin." She looked Bob dead in the eye.

Bob said, "Ari?"

Constance said, "You know his real name's not Lee J. Wilkes."

Bob said, "How well do you know Aronoyad Wilgushku?"

"Well," said Constance.

"Are you the reason he's here? What does he want from you?"

Fine wrinkles compressed her upper lip. "To hurt me. To crush me. To blackmail me. Over a sex tape, if you must know. One of my indiscretions. No doubt, you've heard of others."

"Idle gossip. I pay it no mind," said Bob.

"Bob, my job here is all I care about," said Constance.

"What else does he want?"

"Credit card information. But that's just the beginning."

"Have you given him any?"

"No. I'll see him dead first. He's a bad man. A very bad, very sick man."

A light tap sounded on her door before Mikhail poked his head in.

"Oh, hey, Bob," he said. "Have you seen Vlad?"

"We're in a meeting," said Constance. "Vlad? The cook? Not here. Why on earth would you look for Vlad here?"

"That one stuck," said Bob. "I thought only the maintenance shop called him Vlad."

Mikhail laughed. "No, he likes it. He won't even answer to his real name, anymore."

"Come in and shut the door, Mikhail," said Constance. "Please, shut the door."

"I'll be moseying on," said Bob, rising to his feet.

"Stay, Bob, please," said Constance.

Bob sat back down.

"Mikhail, tell Bob what you threatened to do with that video you took with your phone."

Mikhail started to mumble gibberish.

With her hands against her cheeks, Constance mocked him with big round saucers for eyes, "He threatened to put it on the internet!" Her instant of whimsy disappeared like vapor.

"And what if I tell Ari that you, Mikhail, are the greatest lover, the most virile, rock hardest man I ever had? What do you think Ari will say to that?"

"Please don't," said Mikhail. "Connie, please. Never joke like that."

Constance narrowed her eyes. "What did you do to Uncle Raleigh?"

"Nothing, I swear," said Mikhail.

She shook her finger in his face. "You poisoned him. What did you bring him?"

Mikhail cowered under her fury. "Soup. I brought him soup."

"Who gave you soup for him? Ari? Ari?"

Mikhail hung his head. He dissolved in tears.

"Get out," Constance snarled. "Shut the door behind you."

Mikhail wiped his eyes and skulked out of the room.

"Sorry you had to see that," she said. "I'm so not embarrassed."

Constance leaned back in her chair, suddenly more at ease with Bob than she had ever been. "I'm not going to let that son of a bitch take over my hotel."

When her attention returned to him, Bob said, "You are queen of the carnies."

"Maybe I am," said Constance. "People expect me to make decisions. I can have help here in two hours. Is it time to make the call yet? I don't think so."

Bob said, "Help from Uncle Raleigh's minions?"

"They answer to me now," said Constance.

Bob nodded. "We appear to be in concordance, Constance."

Constance smiled. "Bob, you said my name. You've never said my name before."

"Surely, I must have," said Bob.

"I don't think so," said Constance. "I'm sure you have a pet nickname for me that you prefer."

"None that ever stuck," said Bob.

CHAPTER NINETEEN
ROOFERS

Back at the shop, two old roofers from Chipton Roofing had arrived to patch the roof. As cavalier about their futile mission as it was possible to be, they slouched and shuffled into the shop to consult with Ed Nogg about the most pervasive leaks.

The older one with the pronounced limp, rolled an unlit cigarette around in his loose lips and mumbled, "That old roof's seen better days."

"I know it has," said Ed.

Linwood Chipton balled his fists in the pockets of his faded jeans and shook his head. "Don't reckon it's ever a good time to mention a new roof, is it?"

"No, sir, especially not today," said Ed.

"Alright, then," said Linwood. "We'll patch her up."

The other old roofer followed him out of the shop.

Ed looked up from his email monitoring mode and watched them go. He shared a look with Bob and shook his head. "Every time they come out here, it costs about four hundred and fifty bucks."

Bob had the gift of saying nothing when nothing needed to be said. He was occupied repairing a three-way desk lamp and somehow managed with nods to carry on a conversation with Ed.

"How you holding up, little buddy?" Ed asked, when he finally got around to asking.

"Never better," said Bob.

"You had a nice little chat with David?"

"Yes, we bonded," said Bob.

"Good," said Ed. "You know, he likes you, Bob."

"Is that good or bad from where you sit?"

"From where I sit, it's real good," said Ed. "I'm not jealous, if that's what you mean. Just because I've had my nose up his ass for four years doesn't mean he has to like me."

"They also serve who only stand and wait," said Bob.

Ed laughed loud and long. He said, "Bob, where do you get this stuff? We need to find you a friend."

Ed had suggested on prior occasions that Bob might want to meet some of his wife's single friends. Bob treated all such suggestions as polite chatter, but Ed still seemed to think it was an option on the table.

The condescension rolled off Bob's back like nothing, as if someday he might take him up on it, just not today.

"Bob, do me a favor, please," said Ed, "will you check the water level in the courtyard fountain? David sent an email, says it looks low."

•　　•　　•　　•　　•　　•

As Bob was checking the fountain, he sighted Claudia walking along the ocean strand with Lee J. Wilkes. She was talking, and he was listening.

Bob looked away. Waking out of his darkest nights, he would see her prancing toward him in slow motion or running beside him down the long empty beach into the first rays of sunrise. In those running dreams with her, he was her champion.

The water level in the fountain adjusted, Bob watched Claudia and Lee J. Wilkes turn and begin to stroll back toward the Lodge. Bob noted how gracefully Wilkes arm around her shoulder had swept her off her feet like the wind and swung her around to the opposite direction.

Aronoyad had all the moves.

Next, Bob was called to unclog a plugged sink line at the Oasis outdoor poolside oceanfront restaurant bar, the one sink line that regularly clogged with plastic straws, toothpicks, cherry stems and tiny plastic cutlasses.

As Bob inspected the plugged sink from behind and underneath the bar, Claudia and Lee J. Wilkes strolled up from the beach and took chairs at the bar. They ordered drinks and Wilkes bought rounds for everyone in sight. Bob knew an awkward moment was soon to come when he would stand up with bar sink sludge on his hands and have to look or not look at Claudia to see if she was looking or not looking at him. It was all so tedious.

Always the same dirty, messy job that somebody had to do – clear out the grease and gunk in the line. Most important was running hot water through the cleared line for a few minutes once a day, which no one ever did.

When Bob stood up from under the sink, Claudia was seated directly across the bar from him. He started running hot water down the drain and had to stand there watching it drain. Claudia smiled at Bob and Wilkes said, "How we doing, Bob?"

Bob looked at Wilkes without answering.

The hot water raised a cloud of steam in the sink as the bartender stood by to Bob's left and waited.

"I guess it's alright," said Bob, after about twenty seconds. He turned off the water, gathered his tools in a bucket and wiped his work area clean with a towel.

"Thanks, Bob," said the bartender.

"Well done, Bob," said Claudia.

Those were the first words she had ever spoken to him directly, but he had no time to savor them before Wilkes also congratulated him on a job well done.

"Good, Bob. Very good."

Oh, the indignity.

Bob felt ashamed of himself, to be nursing his wounded pride yet again. Enough. There were worse scenarios than social humiliation.

And yet, if it were possible, he would almost have rather died protecting Claudia from Aronoyad Wilgushku, than live with the shame of having done nothing to stop him.

Still later that day at the Oasis, after Claudia had departed, Wilkes, having made friends with the bartender, Nick, had learned a bit of the history of the Lodge. He'd noticed the two old roofers on the roof, maneuvering around on the tiles, replacing the flashing on one of the chimneys. They looked way too old to be up that high with no ropes or safety harnesses.

"OSHA would shut this hotel down if they saw them up there with no safety lines," said Wilkes.

Nick nodded, then said, "Hello, Mr. Moriarty," as David took a stool next to Wilkes. Nick poured a glass of cranberry juice over ice and set it down on a coaster in front of David.

David extended a hand to Mr. Wilkes. "Hi, I'm David Moriarty. As General Manager of the Lodge and Club, I want to extend a personal welcome to our newest Club member, Mr. Lee J. Wilkes, I presume."

"Thank you, David. Please call me Ari."

"Ari?"

"Yes, informal is best. Allow me to buy you a drink, sir."

"Well," said David, looking at his watch, "I don't really drink, but allow me to buy you one."

"What does 'really' drink mean?" said Wilkes. "If you don't drink, say you don't drink, don't say you don't really drink. It's an indecisive equivocation."

"I never really thought of it that way," said David.

"Really?" Ari beamed the light of his full attention on David. "Let's have a drink."

David surprised himself by accepting the offer.

Nick the bartender would later say that he had never seen David laugh before, or drink alcohol before, or talk as much to any one person.

David even talked about the roof with Wilkes.

Wilkes insisted on supplying a roofer. His men would do a better job, he said, than those old timers up there with no safety lines. David demurred, but Wilkes guaranteed extraordinary and immediate results.

"Nothing ever works for long," said David. "They patch the patches, and they leak again."

"There are ways," said Wilkes. "My guys know. Try my guys. If you're not satisfied, no charge."

"I can't let you do that," said David.

"It's done," said Wilkes. He held up his phone, poised to dial. "One call."

David shrugged. He looked up. The sky was clear. "First thing tomorrow," he said.

Wilkes made the call. He gave David the thumb up. "All set."

"Not quite," said David, pulling out his own phone. "I have to tell Ed to can those other guys."

"Are they under contract?"

"Probably."

"Safety violation. No harness, no rope. Goodbye."

Nick turned the volume on the TV way down as David dialed the maintenance shop extension. Ed Nogg picked up on the second ring.

"Yes, David."

"Hey, Ed. Um, listen, about these roofers. They're up there climbing around on the roof with no safety harness or ropes. I'm pretty sure that's a breach of contract if it violates safety standards. So I took the liberty, I want to try these new guys. They're coming tomorrow to work on the leaks. So you can tell Linwood Chilton not to come back tomorrow."

"Okay, David," said Ed.

"Thank you, Ed." David hung up.

"Everything good?" said Wilkes.

"I never feel right talking to him," said David. "It always feels like he's blowing smoke up my ass."

"Maybe he thinks that's part of his job," said Wilkes.

"Maybe so," said David. "If it is, I don't like it any more than he does."

"You can tell him that, can't you?"

"No, we're not going there."

"Where shall we go then, David, you and I, in this, our first conversation? College life? What was your field of study?"

"Accounting."

"And before that, what was your passion? Nobody starts out wanting to be an accountant."

"I did," said David. "Always had a thing for numbers."

"Music theory did not interest you?"

"Music theory did interest me very much," said David.

"Numbers. And your passion for music came first, before your passions for numbers and accounting."

"Yes. I always loved music."

"Your instrument, piano?"

"A bit," said David. "I never pursued it."

"Come. We go to piano bar upstairs. You play us a song."

"I don't think so," said David.

"Mr. Moriarty, if you please, sir, spend a few more minutes with me. I consider it an honor to hear you play."

"Whoa," said David. "You almost make me want to hear myself."

Nick transferred Wilkes' bar tab to the Innlet Lounge. Wilkes and David stood together. David smoothed his suit, and they accompanied each other to the lobby elevator.

Pete, the Innlet bartender, had fresh drinks at the ready when the elevator doors opened. Wilkes steered David to the piano and Pete poured David's cranberry juice on ice down the sink.

Pete had known David for a long time. He had heard the rumor that David could play, but he had never heard him play piano before, and no one else he knew had ever heard him play, either. David was not known to be a drinker, and Pete had never seen him drink an alcoholic beverage. As a drinker, he was an unknown quantity.

In the lounge, the ladies who came every day for High Tea were lingering, eating the last of the cookies and scones and talking in the quiet atmosphere, with the gas fire burning in the fireplace and the ocean outside the windows gently lapping the shore.

The tune that began to roll from David's fingers on the keys was a Steely Dan song called *Haitian Divorce*. David noodled around with it as he tried to remember the verses. All he recalled was the rhythm and the melody and the catchy chorus, *"Papa say, Oh, no! Who's that kinky so and so?"*

Wilkes leaned against the bar and sipped single malt scotch.

"He's good," he said to Pete. "But is he a good accountant?"

"Mr. Moriarty is one of those guys who are good at everything they do," said Pete.

David moved on, riffing through songs, creating a tapestry of segues and non-sequiturs arranged around bits and pieces of song fragments. He was like a radio dial with transitions. One moment, he was singing, *Lavender blue, dilly dilly* like Burl Ives, then he went into the Peter Gunn theme just long enough to leave it and hit the rousing opening theme for Bonanza, to which a rare few knew the words, *We got a hold of a potful of gold, a bonanza ...* He shifted moods easily, dropping down low to mimic a crooning Jerry Lee Lewis, *Hey dollin'...this is the Killer speaking..."*

Some of the high tea ladies stopped talking and turned to see who was at the piano. When they recognized David Moriarty, their expressions changed from annoyance to surprise and for some of them, rapturous joy, except for Mama Muumuu. She sat with her back half turned, scowling, as the ladies at her table billed and cooed over David's bravura performance.

He came trickling back, by way of Erroll Garner, to cap his early Steely Dan medley with *Bad sneakers and a Pina Colada, my friend ...*

Wilkes and Pete applauded as David finished with a rousing send-up of the WKRP closing theme. He stood up with a big smile on his face, leaned over the microphone and said, "I want to send a shout out to all my peeps and homies. Yo. Represent."

Wilkes continued to applaud as David left the piano and came over to take a seat at the bar. "I'll have that drink now," he said.

Pete had one ready for him, cranberry juice and vodka with orange Curacao.

"That was fun," said David.

"You are an entertainer, David," said Wilkes. "You should do a show here."

"To a captive audience? No, that's not for me." He tossed back his drink. "This was special, though. Thank you, Ari. That was the most fun I've had in ... a long time."

"Play some more, Party Boy," said Wilkes.

David forced a pleasant laugh. "Did you just call me Party Boy?"

"Sorry, Boss," said Wilkes.

"That was my nickname in college," said David. "How would you know that?"

"Spooky," said Wilkes.

David looked at his watch. "I have to go," he said. "Maybe I'll see you here tomorrow, same time, alright?"

"I bring the cocaine," said Wilkes.

David shot him a flashing look of panic, but Wilkes jocular manner reassured him.

"Just kidding," he said.

David looked around and saw no reason not to laugh. "You got me that time," he said.

Wilkes stood and shook David's hand. "It has been a rare pleasure meeting the real David Moriarty."

"Likewise," said David.

When he was gone, Pete said to Wilkes, "You got closer to him just now than anyone ever has."

"It's a gift," said Wilkes.

CHAPTER TWENTY
GOLDEN TICKET

Linwood Chipton took the news of his firm's termination of services with unflappable panache. "Well, call us if you need us," he said.

Ed had wrestled with his conscience over the message handed down to him from the mountaintop. As furious as he was with David, he could let none of that spill over into his interactions with his staff or with outside contractors. In theory, he was able to compartmentalize his feelings of outrage and resentment, but in reality, those compartments were ram-packed to overflowing, and some of that shit was destined to roll downhill.

For David to toss down a fiat from on high was not unusual. Contractors came and went, along with favored status. But David, as a rule, did not involve himself in the day to day business of the Maintenance Department. He did his walkabouts, made his lists, and dispatched his decrees by email. He was of the mind that if he noticed something awry and mentioned it to Ed, then by the next day, if possible, within reason, the concern should have been addressed.

Some projects, understandably, dragged on. Writing status updates for David kept Ed Nogg chained to his desk. A highly organized individual, Ed Nogg could put his hands on any invoice, memo, or bill. He knew where to find things and how things worked. And if he didn't know, he could puzzle it out.

Every challenge David had thrown at him Ed had handled. And he wouldn't just put it on his staff, he would do the work himself, if that's what it took to get it done. Ed's attitude, upon being hired some five and a half years earlier, was that he could handle any challenge. By demonstrating that can-do initiative, Ed Nogg had committed himself, to his own detriment, to always going the extra mile upon request, to performing miracles of ingenuity and craft above and beyond the managerial parameters of his job description as Facilities Director. The fact that he consistently saved the company money on outsourced contract labor and was under budget every year resulted in his budget being cut even more. The more initiative he showed, the more his talents were taken for granted, and the more he was expected to do. But that was never much of a surprise. Ed could handle David's fits of pique, his peremptory tones. He had not become a Master Chief in the U.S. Navy without learning how to deal with petty ego problems.

Right or wrong, the shit all rolled downhill. Ed took David's walkabout lists and other lists and made his own master lists of tasks, projects and missions. These became work orders distributed to his staff via specific to-do lists. Sometimes, Ed would unload on Karl a barrage of painting orders. Karl would sputter and fume, but Ed was just relieving the pressure, releasing the logjam, letting the massive blockage drop and roll downhill as God and man and nature intended, so that Karl would continue to be driven by the same forces that drove Ed to prove his worth anew each day, as if yesterday neither existed nor mattered, and all work, however excellent today, was to be taken for granted tomorrow and forgotten.

Karl was more volatile than the average Lodge employee. Years of self-employment had left him somewhat unmalleable, and he had yet to get his mind right, as the saying went. There were certain things about the Lodge that everyone got used to. One was the suffocating boredom. Another was the suffocating boredom of having the same exact conversations every day. Karl didn't fish, play golf, or watch football much. There was nothing for Karl to talk about with Ed other than work. It wasn't easy for Karl to have a boss like Ed. And it wasn't easy for Ed being Karl's boss.

A couple of times, Ed had almost fired him for excessive profanity, but Karl was a highly skilled painter and, as much as Ed hated to admit it, he knew the Lodge could not easily replace him, so Ed allowed Karl a slightly wider berth, against his better judgment.

U.S. Navy discipline was the touchstone of Ed's management style, and Karl had made it clear that he was not in the navy. He had never served in the armed forces and continued to feign ignorance of military time.

Karl required civilian treatment, and Ed's resentment over that simmered on low most of the time. It seemed unfair to Ed that Karl, as the sole painter on staff, showed no interest in becoming a well-rounded maintenance man. Whenever Ed sensed in Karl the rise of that lofty attitude, he could not help himself; he had to try to squelch it. He knew no other way.

Having Bob in the shop was a different experience altogether. Ed and Bob never clashed. They functioned together like master and pupil. Bob, the oldest student in the college of maintenance, was also the fastest learner. He absorbed all the knowledge Ed had to offer.

With Karl and Bob both in the shop when the roofers were dismissed, Ed solicited their comments.

"What do you think about all that, Karl?" Ed asked.

"What, letting the Chipton roofers go?"

"Yeah. Who are these new guys? David didn't even give me a name. They're just supposed to show up tomorrow."

"Does he do that much, order you to use a particular contractor?"

"He's never just flat out stepped on my toes like that before," said Ed.

"It does seem weird," said Karl.

"What do you think, Bob?" said Ed.

"I don't think, I feel," said Bob.

"Well, I don't mind telling you guys," said Ed, "it chaps my ass, but it makes me wonder what is going on with David. He does not want to get involved in my day to day business."

• • •• • •• •• ••

On his way home that afternoon, Bob placed a semi-secure call to Berne Ventine.

"Hello, Bob," said Berne. "You've had an interesting couple of days, haven't you?"

"Whom the gods would destroy, they first make mad," said Bob.

"Now, Bob, don't be hifalutin' all the time. I know you're a big reader, but I'm not playing 'name that quote' with you. Longfellow, by the way."

"Berne, he's here."

"I know."

"What kind of parole is that where he leaves the state and lives like a sultan at a hotel under a false identity?"

"Bob, do you really have to ask?" said Berne.

"Berne, everything you've told me so far has been a day late. Your loyalties appear to be divided," said Bob.

"I'm looking out for you, Bob. My loyalties are not divided. You still want out, I got you down for West Bunkie. You can leave tonight. If that's what you want to do."

"I'd rather die with my boots on here," said Bob.

"You don't have to die. It's under control, I promise."

"You've got the Lodge under surveillance?"

"Oh, yeah," said Berne. "Say, we found a few of those EMP emitters in Featherton's room. Sweet."

"Who's behind Wilkes now that Featherton's dead? He's got a golden ticket here."

"I'll tell you one thing, Bob," said Berne. "He does not have a golden ticket, whatever you think that is."

"He bought a membership today," said Bob, "plunked down twenty grand to become a member of a fitness club for wealthy retirees. Don't tell me that's his cash. He said he's not here to kill me, so what's he here for? What does he want?"

"What everyone wants," said Berne, "love. Another chance to make things right. Everybody wants that. Don't tell me they don't."

"Are you his handler?"

"No. And everything I've told you is classified. I had no authority to share it with you."

"You haven't told me anything," said Bob.

"Ask the right questions."

"Is my daughter's family safe?"

"Yes."

"Am I going to be arrested?"

"No charges have been filed. Featherton died of a heart attack. The Senator committed suicide. Relax, you might get through this."

"How committed are you to Ari?"

"Not committed at all," said Berne.

"Was that the right question?"

"Good night, Bob."

The next day, the new roofers didn't show up early. By mid-morning they still had not shown up, and Ed was getting antsy. Bob and Karl stayed busy with their lists while Ed smoldered in front of his computer screen, composing emails to David that he ultimately would not send, not if he wanted to keep his job, which he did, although it entailed more bullshit than he'd encountered in twenty years of military service.

By noon, the roofers had still not shown and Ed could stand it no longer.

"I'm meeting my wife for lunch," he said. "I might not come back. I think I need to drain my pool."

"Want me to tell David the new roofers haven't shown?" said Bob.

"Would you mind? I don't trust myself to talk to David right now," he said.

Ed left and did not return that day. By one o'clock, the roofers had still not shown, and Bob was about to call David Moriarty's office when the phone rang. It was David calling to ask for a status report on the new roofers.

"I was just about to call you," said Bob. "The new roofers have yet to show."

"They what?"

"They have not shown up yet," said Bob.

"Why wasn't I told?" David's inner princess took it as a personal affront.

"Well, we want to give them every opportunity," said Bob, "to overcome a less than stellar first impression."

"They were supposed to be here this morning, Bob. First thing this morning."

"I know."

"I'll call you back," said David.

David called Wilkes' room. He was not in. David left his office and crossed the street to the Lodge and found Wilkes at the Oasis Bar.

Wilkes wore a beach shirt, sunglasses and beach togs. He welcomed David with open arms, but David held him off with a vertical palm.

"Your roofers haven't shown up," said David. "I put myself out for you."

"My guys not here yet?" Wilkes' incredulity nearly deflected David's ire.

"I had my maintenance supervisor fire the other roofers on your say-so, something I never should have done, but I did it because you vouched for your roofers. So, where are they? It's one thirty," said David.

"Whoa, David, whoa," said Wilkes, "let me get to the bottom of this. I apologize. It's my fault. I make one call." He speed-dialed a number and was speaking within seconds in a language known to very few. He closed the phone and smiled at David.

"They are here now. They are pulling into the garage at this very moment."

"Now," said David. "They're here now."

"They had some lateness at another job, some problem. I apologize."

"I don't like uncertainty," said David.

* * *

The new roofers arrived in a beat up white pickup truck with a bucket of tar and several rolls of tar paper in the back, along with some shovels and hand tools. No official logo on the truck. The leader of the three-man crew was a tall young kid in his early twenties with no shirt on and tattoos all over his chest and arms. The black guy and the Mexican were older.

The trio arrived ready to go to work at one-thirty in the afternoon. Bob was not inclined to even let them get started, but it was not his decision to make.

Karl took the initiative and told the kid that he had to wear a shirt.

"I got one," the kid assured him. He indicated an orange T-shirt hanging like a rag from the belt loop of his jeans.

"You have to wear it," said Karl.

"I will," said the kid.

"You have to put it on now," said Karl, "and wear it the whole time you're here."

"Dude, okay," said the kid, pulling the orange shirt free of its loop and shaking out the wrinkles. He pulled on the shirt. "Okay?"

"You got a safety rope?" Bob asked.

"Uh, what?"

"A safety rope?"

"Yeah, yeah, we got one," said the kid.

"What's the name of your company?" Karl asked.

"Red Door Roofing."

CHAPTER TWENTY-ONE
THE FALLEN

Detective Billy Carlisle had just about wrapped up his investigation. His conclusions were in his report, which was not quite finished yet because his notes were still in the pocket of his jacket, hanging in the closet in Shania Doyle's bedroom. He knew a little more now than he had known a couple of days ago about the Lodge homicides. He knew they were not listed as homicides. And he knew that there was no one in the Belle Rive County Sheriff's office waiting to read his official report.

He knew he would be fired for crossing the line with a reporter, unless he quit first. At that red hot moment, though, his profession was not his priority. Pleasing Shania was more important, and so far, she was pleased.

He had shared confidential information with her, and she had used it in her article to debut on the crime beat of their local paper. From the start, Billy had thought that they had something going on that was better than that. It just was.

She would wake up horny like the woman of his dreams and snap off quick, sharp, explosive orgasms like a string of firecrackers. That made him so hot. He told her, "Babe, if you're faking, keep doing it."

She said, "No, Bill. You please me."

All he wanted after that was to keep his dick in her all the time.

But they had to eat, so they were getting breakfast. Both liked the full meal deal, omelet, bacon, sausage, pancakes. They scarfed so easily together. That had to mean something.

Billy knew the truth was going to continue to eat at him until it finally sank into his gut that the chemistry they had together was casual sex to her, nothing more.

It meant everything to him. It was God giving him a taste of true happiness just to snatch it away. But, he told himself, just because it hadn't been snatched away yet didn't mean it wasn't meant to last.

Yes, it was going to ravage him when she was gone, but for now no price was too high to keep her, certainly not his job.

The Belle Rive County Sheriff's Department would hardly miss him. He was their one homicide investigator, but they had no homicides. Belle Rive County basically had no crime. They had speeders and other traffic violators. When they did have a homicide, they jumped at the chance to call it accidental death or suicide. Scandalous shit happened elsewhere; not in Belle Rive County.

Billy Carlisle couldn't say he didn't know what to expect when he took the job of Homicide Investigator in a county with no homicides. He had known it would be a soul killer. He'd hoped to be able to change things. Instead, he had changed, growing accustomed to the routine of doing nothing all day, practically nothing at first, then, after a while, absolutely nothing.

He was pushing forty. He'd been a cop for eighteen years. In two years, he could retire with a pension, do something else. It wasn't too late to start a family.

Shania was fifteen years younger and nowhere near ready to be tied down. Billy was able to accept that in theory. But letting her go was unthinkable.

"Billy," she said, "what are we going to do?"

"About what?" said Billy, knowing she didn't mean "about us."

"You really don't care, do you?"

"I do, babe, but the bullshit is neck deep."

"No one's going to solve this case if we don't," said Shania.

"It's not even a case," said Billy. "There's no murder."

"We need to go back to the Lodge and talk to some of those people again."

"Who, that bitch?"

"She said she and Featherton weren't close, but she inherits."

"Your story's still dead in the water," said Billy.

"Plus, she lied about Bob. Why'd she throw him under the bus? She said he was acting weird."

"You don't think Bob was acting weird that day?"

"Bob didn't do anything."

"Shot her uncle with a nail gun."

"Who happened to be a crime lord. Why would Bob to do that?"

"Poor impulse control," said Billy, hoping to get a chuckle out of her.

"Something's going on at the Lodge," said Shania.

Billy didn't want to keep any more secrets.

"The Lodge is under surveillance," he said. "Has been for days."

Shania perked up. "By the Federales?"

"Listen to you, the Federales." Billy tried joshing her, "Watch a lot of westerns, do you?"

"Witness Protection," Shania guessed. "The Marshals Service. I'm right, aren't I? You knew, you just didn't want to say."

"Well, excuse me for not blurting it out," said Billy.

"If Bob's in WitSec," said Shania, "where'd he come from?"

"Let's not worry about that now," said Billy. "Can we talk about us for a minute?"

Shania dialed Constance's number. "Not now," she said.

Alone in her office, Constance experimented with the handwritten registration card of Lee J. Wilkes. It was easy enough to copy his signature, quite another to extrapolate from that a handwriting sample. If she were to pen an incriminating note on a comment card, it might suggest him becoming erratic or suicidal. Then she could kill him. She couldn't let him get away with hurting her again. Maybe a list of his aliases. The comment card would alert the Human Resources Director, Martina Crabshaw, whose office in the administration building was right next to David's. Martina would bring the card to David and, whether he believed the information or not, he would not be able to ignore it. David would know that Wilkes was dangerous, but too late.

It was a crazy plan. Not a good one. Constance had nothing else. She knew she couldn't count on David Moriarty or Martina Crabshaw as lifelines. They would never even know who they were up against. Constance was going to have to handle Aronoyad herself.

Her phone rang. The reporter, Shania Doyle, wanted to meet with her again. Constance agreed to meet with her off property for lunch.

Cruiser's Grill had quiet booths in the back that weren't bustling with the lunchtime trade. Shania followed a waitress back and took a seat across from Constance.

"Thank you for meeting with me," Shania said. She picked up a pen.

"I won't go on record for a story like your last one," said Constance. "If you quote me, I might be killed."

"Killed?" said Shania.

Constance eyed the pen still in her hand. Shania set it down.

"What are you willing to tell me?"

"Not much," said Constance. "I don't see how you can help me. Since I don't want my story written."

"Then I won't write your story," said Shania.

"So you say," said Constance. She sipped her iced tea. "You don't know anything, do you? I'd have to start at the beginning. I can't do that."

"Start in the middle," said Shania, "start anywhere. Just start. I'll catch up."

"My Uncle Raleigh was well connected. You know what that means?"

"I've been to the movies," said Shania.

"It's different down south," said Constance. "The Featherton circuit reaches from Tampa to Little Rock. For fifty years, Uncle Raleigh ran carnivals all over the country while he traveled the world, trading in currencies, art and information. He was more global than regional, but he kept his territory intact. His hobby was collecting data about people with massive fortunes. He followed their investments and knew who all their heirs were. He kept files on Very Important People with sons and daughters in rehab. There are only a handful of exclusive rehab clinics scattered around the world qualified to handle extremely wealthy high maintenance patients."

"And you were privy to your great uncle Raleigh's secret hobbies and financial affairs?"

"He had no other heir," said Constance.

"Were you groomed to be his heir?"

"From an early age," said Constance. "But I'm not going there. Uncle Raleigh kept track of the wealthiest people. He knew where the largest fortunes were, and where they were most vulnerable. He specialized in that specific kind of information."

Shania placed a small digital recorder on the table. "Please," she said.

Constance, caught up in her story, paid it no attention.

"He kept his records in coded ledgers. That's what this is all about, the contents of those ledgers. What names are in them? No one knows. When one was stolen, it devastated Uncle Raleigh. That the thief was close to him broke his heart. He loved Ari. He would have made him a prince. And I was the currency of his realm, his princess."

After a long lunch, Shania discovered that she had recorded a lot of white noise.

• • • • •

Karl shared an anecdote with Bob as they rode the golf cart out to the Dumpster at the far end of the gym parking lot. Two bags of trash were loaded in the back bed.

"Someone, as you know, always has to do the dirty work," said Karl, "but I don't mind. I was painting the fireplace mantel yet again, as per David's request. It gets sooty every other day since the problem with the flue."

Bob listened impassively as they rode along.

"King David and the Sultan were huddled over a high top table by the ocean window in the Innlet Bar," said Karl, "trying to keep their voices down. David kept saying 'no' and Wilkes kept saying 'yes.' Then David shushed him. I was too close. They got up and moved to another table. Why'd they sit there in the first place if they needed the Cone of Silence? That seemed to me like a lapse in David's regular behavior pattern. He would have never put himself in that position on purpose, where he could be overheard holding a secretive conversation."

Karl stopped the cart outside the wooden gate and carried a bag of trash up the steps to the landing where the Dumpster door opened. He tossed the bag in and Bob handed the other bag up to him. Karl tossed it in and shut the door, and Bob pushed the button to start the compactor. The hydraulic motor whined through its cycle and stopped.

In the sudden silence, Karl asked, "What's going on, Bob? The Sultan's pimping by the pool all day and all night in the bar, too, I hear. This place is turning into The Satyricon. Is it becoming a swinging singles spot?"

Bob said, "And you ask yourself, is that so terrible?"

Karl shrugged. "This fucking place can't be that easy to take over."

"He hasn't taken over yet," said Bob.

"You see it though, don't you?"

"I see the NQ rising," said Bob.

"The Sultan arrives, rents eight rooms and starts running talent the first night. What kind of gauche motherfucker does that? The motivational speaker leaves his entourage behind with his guru, and they all turn into Stepford hoes. What the fuck is going on? Now he's a member?

Those hookers by the pool aren't members, are they? Or, are they? Not yet. You think he'll be here a year? I don't. Surely he'll realize the folly of his ways."

It was a short ride in the golf cart from the Dumpster back to the shop. Conversations with Karl were often one-sided monologues requiring scant encouragement; a timely chuckle, no more. Bob could respond in no other way. He carried within him an aloofness that was suitable for adaptation and worked well with anonymity and not as well with friends, unless they were friends like Karl who did not mind being kept at arm's length.

It was Bob's way to keep his own counsel. As it was Karl's way to construct scenarios based on suppositions. To each his own.

At the upcoming owners' meeting, to which David Moriarty expected an engraved invitation, the matter of the pending disposition of the builder's five shares was certain to be addressed. The original builder of the Lodge, Shadrach Yelvington, had retained five percentage points of ownership against the current Owner's ninety-five. For personal reasons, as he had announced at the last Owners Meeting, he was considering offering his shares for sale to key management personnel.

David desperately wanted those five points, all five of them. By rights, he felt he should have been offered the shares first as a courtesy, before the feeding frenzy of an auction ensued.

The five shares were not for sale to the majority Owner. They were to be offered first to qualified management personnel. David had the numbers in his head. He had some money set aside for the purchase, but if the shares went to auction, not enough to secure all five.

An auction would bring the higher dollar, but the costs of running an auction along with other mitigating factors argued against the hassle of it all and favored the ease of a private transaction. With little hope that it would go that way, David prepared to bid on the auctioned shares and come away with a hard-won piece of the Lodge.

If he needed more money, he could get it, although not without compromise. The last thing he wanted was to share his shares.

On his daily walkabout, David liked to vary his route and never take the same path twice in a row. Still, he always ended up in the Ocean Room at the north window overlooking the adult pool. He was accustomed to seeing a regular crowd. By regular, he supposed he might have meant mature, or subdued, or quiet. In any case, not rowdy. Even on the biggest days of summer, Memorial Day or the Fourth of July, the teenage children of members behaved appropriately, as a general rule. It was often the friends of friends of members' teenage children that acted up and caused commotion.

The beautiful women and girls around the pool were typically guests and members and daughters and friends of daughters of guests and members. They all shared a certain look. They all belonged. There was no problem with any of them.

The problem was the new professionals, who did not belong.

Nothing at the Lodge escaped David's vigilant eye. Clearly, that was his vanity, but no one was going to run hookers right under his nose at his own hotel. No one.

David watched Wilkes holding court at one of the umbrella-shaded patio tables, cell phone to his ear, loyal minions standing by. Wilkes' ubiquitous presence at either the Innlet Bar or the Oasis was getting annoying, although there had been a good bar crowd lately in both bars in the early evenings. Business had picked up. Beautiful people surrounded the pool. Wealthy guests filled patio lunch tables. The beachfront tableau presented a classy atmosphere, with hookers.

David knew he could not close his eyes to the hookers. He took the staff elevator down and emerged through the Oasis kitchen door.

The women flanking Ari at the Oasis bar were models of sculpted flesh in bikinis and woven wraparounds. Two more in silk string thongs beautified the poolside area, buns of steel glistening with a hand rubbed sheen.

David came up behind Wilkes and tapped him on the shoulder.

Wilkes turned and cast his arms wide to greet David. "David, my friend!"

David said sternly, "Mr. Wilkes, this is the Lodge and Club, not some skanky Casbah."

Wilkes protested, "David, these lovely women are my friends."

"You disappoint me," said David.

Wilkes smiled at David. "These are your guests. Are these women not your guests?"

David turned and walked away. To be confrontational in front of the women disturbed him. No doubt, it was that company sponsored sensitivity training kicking in with its warnings not to say or do anything that might be construed as offensive to women, like calling them hookers.

When he reached the lobby his fury was churning inside him like a bunch of bad decisions trying to bust out of a bag. He was about to call Security, but he realized that would entail talking to Marvin Gardener. That gave him pause. While he hesitated, a Belle Rive County Sheriff's Department patrol car pulled up in front and parked under the porte-cochere.

Detective Carlisle got out of the car, and David stepped forward through the front doors to meet him.

"Good afternoon, Deputy. As you can see this is a fire lane, and we have to keep this thruway open. So, if you would, please pull your vehicle up a bit."

Detective Carlisle strode past David. "I won't be here long," he said.

At the bell stand, Mikhail stood watching as Detective Carlisle stepped up to him with his hand on his firearm.

"Mikhail Bulbek, you are under arrest."

"For what?"

"Extortion and Criminal Conspiracy." He slapped a set of handcuffs on Mikhail, marched him over to the cruiser and tucked him into the back seat.

David walked over to ask Detective Carlisle. "He did what, now?"

The detective shook his head and said, "Not now." He climbed behind the wheel and strapped on his seat belt.

From a construction trailer a few houses down the street where a major renovation was underway, Berne Ventine watched a surveillance monitor replay digital footage of Mikhail's arrest.

"Off script alert," said Berne. "Did that imbecile not get the memo? Billingsley, intercept that cruiser."

"Yes, sir," said the marshal dressed as a construction worker.

He jumped into a green golf cart and zipped down the street. He crossed to the Lodge as Billy's police cruiser eased out from under the porte-cochere. Billingsley blocked his exit with the golf cart. He flashed his badge and came around to the driver's side.

The window rolled down automatically.

"Detective Carlisle, sir, as a professional courtesy, the U.S. Marshals Service requests your immediate cooperation. Please follow me," said the marshal.

Accustomed to his orders being obeyed, Billingsley returned to the golf cart, looked Detective Carlisle in the eye, nodded and caught a nod in return before he backed up and turned around. He led the detective fifty yards up the street and into the shaded driveway of a magnificent oceanfront home. A black Lincoln parked behind the police cruiser, effectively blocking it in.

Billingsley beckoned to Detective Carlisle to exit his vehicle and enter the Lincoln. He opened the door to the back seat and closed it behind him. Berne Ventine sat composed with a drink in his hand. He smiled a cold, sardonic glower.

"Detective Billy Carlisle, headliner." He offered his hand and got the handshake out of the way. "Berne Ventine, U.S. Marshals Service."

"Pleasure," said Detective Carlisle.

"Let's see," said Berne, "where to start? Are you kidding me? We work and slave for months, for years, to build a suitable edifice from which to take the plunge. We're set to launch the biggest sting operation in law enforcement history, and who steps up? Detective Carlisle."

"What got you out of bed this morning, Detective? Making a quick run out for rubbers and suddenly decide to fubar something? That bellman was one of our major assets. Emphasis on 'was.'"

"Well, if you want him that bad, you can have him back," said Detective Carlisle.

"You were seen arresting him. You can't officially hand him over to us because our joint task force is not officially orientated to your local chain of command. Officially. Unofficially, of course, none of this ever happened."

"Well, now that I have your attention, what do you want me to do?"

"How about if you just go on home and keep banging away on that reporter. And maybe not confide in her anymore. You two sleuths are something else. Putting two and two together."

"What about the unsub?"

"Never you mind about the unsub. Go on back to Pleasantville. That's in Dumbassland. You're not in the loop, Detective. I hope I've made myself clear."

Bill said, "In my defense, I was given no heads up whatsoever on your operation. You might want to send out a memo next time."

"The memo's on your desk, Detective Carlisle, under a stack of car catalogs."

CHAPTER TWENTY-TWO
THE FEATHERTON LEDGER

Shania Doyle parked her red Mazda outside Bob's apartment within minutes of his estimated time of arrival home from work. She waited next to his regular parking spot and listened to the radio.

Bob did not return her welcoming smile when he pulled in.

"Hi, Bob," she said, getting out of her car a moment before he did.

Bob was ten steps from his apartment. She walked backwards in front of him, slowing him down.

"Interstate transport of bingo machines," she said. "That's a crime in Alabama?"

Bob dropped his keys back in his pocket. "Incommunicado."

Shania said, "Where can I find Robert Deighton, formerly a corporate executive for RayMor Trucking."

"Deighton was a mid-level manager," said Bob, "a traffic coordinator, not a corporate exec. Get your facts straight."

"Sorry," said Shania. "Vice-President of Transportation sounds like an executive title."

"That's what they'd like you to believe," said Bob.

Shania took a moment. "Larry "the Cherry" Wilhoite, formerly the immigrant boy, Aronoyad Wilgushku, has a new identity, Lee J. Wilkes, and likes to be called Ari. A brightness spread from her Irish eyes to the ironic tone of her voice, "Sentenced to five years for interstate transport of contraband gambling machines," she coughed, "sorry, that part always cracks me up. Wilhoite, aka Wilkes, served four years, was recently paroled and is currently a resident guest in the Presidential Suite at the Lodge while U. S. Marshals have the Lodge under surveillance. Can you connect some of that for me, Bob? Because I'm like, what are the Marshals looking for? And if Ari Wilkes is their boy, what's he after? And what about you, Bob? Are you in danger from this fellow, Aronayad Wilgushku?"

Bob said, "I'm going inside now and I am not inviting you in."

Shania pretended Bob had said that for effect.

"Oh, Bob, I'd so love a drink. I so need a drink."

"That's what bars are for," said Bob.

"I know a great place we can go," she said. "Come with me, Bob."

"No," said Bob. "You go."

Shania put her hand on his arm. "Don't be like that," she said.

Bob pulled his arm away. "I could be your grandfather."

"But, you're not," said Shania.

Bob's next door neighbor poked his head out the door. "I thought I heard voices. Hey, Bob, some of your mail came to my box. I've been out of town so it's a few days old."

"Thanks, Chas, I'll get it later," said Bob.

"Might be important," said Chas. He turned back into his house, leaving his door ajar. He returned with a padded mailer, securely taped.

"Not your birthday, is it?" said Chas.

"No."

"Well, see you." Chas went back inside his apartment and closed his door.

Shania looked at Bob. "There are so many things I could say right now."

"How about goodbye?"

Shania used her smile like a Taser.

"That's tradecraft, baby. Spies do that. One wrong digit, your neighbor gets your package. Know any spies, Bob? Looks like someone sent you a book."

"I like to open my mail in private," said Bob.

Shania patted his cheek. "You'll get used to me, Bob."

Bob fit his key in the lock. "Fair warning. My apartment may be bugged," he said. "Discretion at all times is advisable."

"We'll turn the music up loud," said Shania, pushing past him. She kicked off her shoes and threw herself down on the couch. "I am so tired," she said. "If I could just take a nap."

"Go ahead," said Bob.

She sprang up reflexively, back on her feet. "Just kidding."

Bob poured chilled vodka into two small glasses. "There's cranberry juice if you want it," he said. He set the bottle on the table in the breakfast nook and took a seat. She joined him there. They sat across from each other and clinked glasses.

"Das vedanya," said Bob.

She tossed back her drink and set the glass down for a refill. Bob did the same.

The package lay unopened on the table between them as they scrutinized each other. She didn't look away, and Bob felt himself falling into those green fountains of youth. In the end, all the 'no's' of his life were nullified by one 'yes.'

Bob removed the Gerber handy tool from the holster on his belt and flicked it open with his wrist. A blade extended, and he used it to slice the top flap of the envelope. He extracted a black leather portfolio tied with a purple silk cord and laid it on the table.

Inside the portfolio were two ledgers, one with a matching black leather cover, the other an ordinary bound accounts notebook. Shania crowded close to his shoulder as Bob opened the original and thumbed through its vellum pages covered front to back with coded symbols.

Bob hefted the smaller second ledger, weighed it in hand against the original. The two books looked unrelated, separated by centuries.

Inside the second ledger, he found a single sheet of Lodge stationery addressed to him.

Bob,
We all fall short. Maybe you won't. You inspire me.
James Turner Rutland

The second ledger appeared to be a codex key to the original and included a partial translation. Half its pages were filled with numbers and names.

He stepped back and let Shania see the pages.

Bob poured another drink.

"Hit me," she said. He poured her one.

Her phone was ringing in her purse. The ringtone was the Blondie song, *Call Me.*

"It's Billy," she said. "Bob, I trust him."

"Nyet," said Bob. He scooped up the codex ledger and placed it with the original back inside the portfolio. He tied a slip knot in the purple cord and slid the portfolio back into the padded envelope.

"Such a dramaturge," said Shania.

"Nyetsky," said Bob.

Shania turned her phone off. "Okay, Bob. For now. But you're not alone in this, anymore. It's my story now."

CHAPTER TWENTY-THREE
THE YELVINGTON SHARES

Behind the closed doors of his office, David Moriarty dashed off a series of emails. His walkabouts always identified discrepancies less vigilant eyes had passed over. Were it not for his dedication to detail, the Lodge could slip, as it had slipped before, into a slough of complacency. That slippage could not be allowed to reoccur.

The Lodge had returned under David's leadership from its derelict years of three-diamond status to four-diamond status and for the last five years as General Manager, David had succeeded in maintaining the four-diamond rating for the Lodge, despite the Owners' stranglehold on his budget, despite the budgeteers who would rather patch a leaking ceiling every time it rains than shell out from the profit column for a new roof.

Nobody shared the financial or the political burdens with him. Nobody knew the trouble he'd seen.

His desk was clutter free, with a phone, laptop, and framed photos of his wife and daughter arranged on the mahogany surface. On his glory wall, his framed diplomas hung next to a displayed collection of token ribbons from marathon races, triathlons, and iron man events. He had yet to win, place or show in any of those competitions, but he consistently finished in the front third.

He was forty-two years old and would never run, swim or bike any faster. Winning wasn't the point anymore, not that it ever was. To finish strong was an achievable goal, like the four-diamond rating instead of the five.

When he could stop thinking about the Yelvington shares, he was reminded of the creeping viral influence of Ari Wilkes. Less than a week had passed since Ari's arrival at the Lodge, and already he had brought in hundreds of thousands of dollars in new membership fees. The women David had mistaken for hookers turned out to be models for a photo shoot Ari had booked for a local surf culture catalog. There was a new wave of glamour by the poolside, and many of the members approved.

David opened a drawer in his desk and removed a small vial of white powder. It had come into his possession surreptitiously. He had found it in his pocket, not an occurrence he could easily dismiss.

In college, he had dabbled, inhaled, experimented and earned the nickname, Party Boy. The temptation was not even strong anymore. Yet he got up and locked his office door anyway. He sat back down at his desk and held the crystalline powder up to the light.

Rumors of cocaine circulating at the Lodge were new, very high-quality cocaine.

In the past, it had never been a problem. Most of the members were older, well established, the youngest members mostly leading-edge baby boomers. The recent new members were younger, and the bar crowd lately was considerably younger.

If Ari was behind the drugs, the truth would out soon enough. There was nothing to be gained by making a stink without proof. He couldn't let it interfere with his plan to secure the Yelvington shares, his most immediate mission.

He had considered calling Shad Yelvington just to talk about things and casually bring up the subject of the shares. "About those shares," he might venture to say, "have you got a magic number in mind?"

He had a good idea already what kind of answer to expect. Having played golf with Shad Yelvington, he knew him to be cantankerous, argumentative, uncooperative, surly and disagreeable. He was rich enough to tool around in a Bugatti and play poker with Duncan Upton, the billionaire majority owner of the Lodge. And he was a good enough poker player to keep his five shares out of Upton's hands.

David turned the photos of his wife and daughter face down on the desk, took out his wallet and removed a credit card and his crispest, newest bill. He rolled the bill into a cylinder, unscrewed the cap of the vial and tapped out a bump onto his laptop cover. With the card, he chopped and shaped the bump into a line.

The procedure was like riding a bike. It all came flooding back to him in waves of reckless memories. He stared at the line for a moment, and tapped out a little more and made two equal lines. He stared at the lines for another long moment, weighing the years of discipline and abstinence against the rush of the boogaloo. It had been so long since a walk in the moonlight.

He made a cursory sign of the cross and hoovered up both lines.

Immediately, he heard the thrumming bass line of his soul awaken.

The phone rang before his initial rush was over. "Oh, shit," he said.

He recognized Mrs. Hanratty's number.

Mrs. Hanratty called regularly to complain about the temperature of the pool. She swam laps and came equipped with her own thermometer to keep her own independent daily record of the pool's fluctuating temperatures.

The lap pool temperature was stabilized at a constant eighty-four degrees. Give or take a degree or two, as water circulated through pumps and drains and was replenished, it remained at or near the mean temperature of eighty-four degrees Fahrenheit, year-round. In the hot months, the temperature sometimes rose as high as eighty-seven. Mrs. Hanratty would complain if it reached eighty-six. In the winter, if it dropped to eighty-two, she would call David and complain that the water was too cold.

David picked up the phone and greeted her with the warmth of long practice.

"Good afternoon, Mrs. Hanratty, how are you today?"

"David, the water in the pool is unbearably hot. It's eighty-seven degrees, for goodness sake."

"I'll take care of it," said David.

"What exactly will you do?" she asked.

"I'll toss a bag of ice in there if that's what it takes," he said.

"Will that work?" She sounded doubtful.

"I don't know," said David. "Do you think it will?"

"There must be other, more standard ways," she said.

"We'll figure something out," said David. "Not to worry, I'll take care of it."

"David," said Mrs. Hanratty, "is something wrong?"

"With the pool pumps? No, everything's fine. If anything's wrong, we'll fix it."

"I mean with the Lodge, David. I've been a member here twenty-one years. And I've seen some things here lately I never thought I'd see. Here at the Lodge. Some unsavory characters, I'll leave it at that. I don't feel safe anymore. Street trash in the locker room, pickpockets. Who are all these new members? Isn't there supposed to be a Review Board? I'm sure that's in the charter."

"Mrs. Hanratty," said David, "you called about the temperature in the pool, and I appreciate your concern about that one thing, but pool temperature is an entirely different issue than not feeling safe at the Lodge anymore because of pickpockets and unsavory characters."

"Yes, but what do you plan to do about it? That's my question."

"I'd much rather deal with the pool temperature first," said David, "and get that taken care of for you. One thing at a time."

"When would be a better time to discuss these other issues, David? I represent a few members with similar concerns. I've known you a long time, David. You can talk to me. Are you sure you're not in some kind of trouble?"

"Mrs. Hanratty, I take the security concerns of all our members very seriously, and I promise to look into those you've mentioned, but for now, why don't I just throw a gram of ice in the pool and we can let that be that until tomorrow."

"A gram of ice?" said Mrs. Hanratty.

"A bag," said David, "a bag of ice."

"David, you're being evasive," said Mrs. Hanratty.

"Mrs. Hanratty, you're trying to seduce me," said David.

"Oh, for goodness sake."

"I'm a happily married man."

"David. You scamp. Stop that right now."

"No, you stop right now," said David.

"Okay, David. Have your little moment. Until tomorrow."

"Thank you for bringing these issues to my attention," said David.

When he hung up, David looked around at the four walls of his office. "Is there anything else I can do for you, today?" he said.

•   •   •

In the Innlet dining room, the head waiter, Renaldo, escorted Mr. Yelvington to the window table where Ari Wilkes awaited his guest. Wilkes rose from his seat and shook his hand.

"Mr. Yelvington," said Wilkes.

"Call me Shad."

"Shad. I am Ari Wilkes."

Ari held up two fingers, and Renaldo disappeared.

The two men settled into the comfortable leather chairs and waited for their drinks to arrive. Outside the large curved windows, a placid gray ocean lapped against the coquina shore. An array of blue beach umbrellas and chairs staked out ample and cozy spaces across the expanse of manicured sand.

"A bustling trade," said Ari.

"Always is, this time of year," said Shad.

"This is a very special location," said Ari, "in this private place, this beautiful building."

"Thank you," said Shad. "The old girl's held up rather well."

Renaldo brought their drinks and withdrew. Neither man glanced at the menus.

"I wonder," said Ari, "how different this hotel would be in South Florida."

"Less conservative," said Shad.

Ari agreed. "Far less."

"People like it quiet around here. They go to bed early," said Shad.

"I have a vision of this hotel attracting the jet set like South Beach in Miami. Hollywood types need a place to get away to where people will leave them alone, a quiet place like this private resort, five-diamond all the way. It could happen."

"The reason The Lodge can't be five-diamond is because the rooms are too small, not the suites, the regular rooms," said Shad.

"Smaller furniture," said Ari.

"Wouldn't that be easy," said Shad.

"I could make this hotel five-diamond," said Ari.

"Mr. Wilkes, you know my five shares are not on the open market," said Shad.

Ari nodded. He said, "I understand. You and Mr. Duncan Upton are very old friends."

Shad leaned back and picked up the menu. He opened it and glanced at it and closed it and put it back on the table. "We go back."

Renaldo returned, took their orders and departed.

Wilkes said, "Mr. Duncan Upton has offered many times to buy your shares, and you refuse to sell to him."

"I keep those five shares just to fuck with him," said Shad.

Ari smiled broadly. "That amuses me enormously," he said. "You are the gadfly in Mr. Upton's ointment."

Shadrach Yelvington nodded. Ari Wilkes understood.

"I don't know anything about his ointments," said Shad, "but the gadfly part is right."

"And you hope to find someone to carry on your tradition."

Shad's shoulder lifted, a mild shrug. "It's a long shot," he admitted.

"But who will bid against David? Risk their job for shares? Why not just sell to David?"

"Wouldn't be fair," said Shad.

"Will you break up the block of five?"

"No, sir. All five shares or nothing."

Ari looked out over the water through the glass. Cirro-nimbus formations in the shimmering haze were turning pink. "I tell you," said Ari, "Mr. Yelvington, sir, builder of this fine hotel, I would like nothing better, and nothing more, than to be the gadfly of this hotel."

David Moriarty breezed into the dining room and headed straight for their table. He was grinning, waving jazz hands, half-dancing and half-singing, "Shadrach, the Shadifier, the Shadillac, how we doing? Shadrach bo-bad rack, bonanabana bo-be-back, be-hind-my-me-shack, Shadrach."

"Hello, David," said Shad, granting David a little golf clap.

Ari winked at David.

"What kind of mischief you cooking up here?" David's right knee bounced like he couldn't keep it still.

"Ain't misbehaving," said Shad, "checking the surf." His little smile grew distant.

David glanced out the window at the flat sea. "Not much out there today," he said.

He stood as Renaldo returned with their entrees on a tray. "Well, I don't mean to intrude on your lunch, gentlemen. Enjoy." David stepped back as he turned and collided with Mama Muumuu, who had arrived for the weekly Bridge session in the Ocean Room.

"Ow!" Mama Muumuu fretted.

"I'm so sorry, Mrs. Canebrake," David said, solicitously taking her elbow, "are you alright, dear?"

"I'll be fine," she said, mollified somewhat by David knowing her proper name.

David walked her out of the dining room, smiling over his shoulder with his teeth clamped together.

Shad said, "I never knew he's such a cutup."

"David is very smart man," said Ari.

"Yes, he is," said Shad.

"Is he not the logical one to buy your shares?"

Shad's little smile turned inside itself, like a caterpillar trying to crawl back into the chrysalis. He studied Ari with a darkened eye.

He said, "You've got a funny way about you, mister."

"I mean no offense," said Ari. "It comes with being prescient."

"Prescient, eh? You see my future?"

"No," said Ari, solemnly.

"Because I don't have one," said Shad.

Ari nodded. "You are prepared."

"Yes, I am," said Shad. "Prepared. So when Mr. Entitlement thinks he deserves first crack at my shares, it hits me wrong. I'd just as soon keep them, or sell them to somebody else right from under his nose. I don't care. Sometimes I feel like shaking things up. I don't want to see them all roll away to Upton, but if they do, they do. I'm done hassling with them."

"Someday I will own those shares," said Ari. "Then I will be the gadfly."

"Be my guest," said Shadrach Yelvington.

CHAPTER TWENTY-FOUR
TRIANGULATE

Bob woke in the middle of the night on the couch. His own couch. With Shania softly snoring in his bed. Shania. Softly snoring. In his bed.

He had no choice. Gentlemanly conduct dictated guardianship. He had insisted on taking the couch, and she had let him. His loaded weapon was on the coffee table. The noise that woke him was a pounding on his front door.

Bob knew it was Detective Bill Carlisle before he opened his eyes.

He snatched up the pistol on the way to the door. Another pound.

"Let me in, Bob. Don't leave me out here."

Bob slid the deadbolt back and opened the door. Bill Carlisle stood with his snap-brim hat in hand.

"It's four o'clock," said Bob. "What?"

Bill said, "Bob, you know she's with me."

Bob said, "She will shred you like wheat. You might as well face it."

"Don't say that to me." Bob stepped back as Bill brushed past him.

Bob flipped on the kitchen light and started to make a pot of coffee. "I'm on the couch," he said.

"I see that," said Bill. He moved down the short hall and opened the bedroom door and saw Shania asleep in her clothes. He started to back away.

She opened her eyes. "Bill?"

"Baby, please," he said, "wait."

She sat up. "What are you doing here? I can't believe you. If you hurt him …"

"I didn't feel like waiting around for three more hours in the parking lot," he said.

"You have no right to stalk me," said Shania, "to follow me …"

"Baby, please," said Bill. "Please don't talk yet, please."

"Don't shush me."

Bob willed his coffee pot to perk faster. He was due for a new coffee pot, one with an automatic sensor. "Let him speak," he said.

"Thanks, Bob," said Bill. "Baby, I am not jealous of this old man."

Bob jerked the coffee pot off the burner with his left hand and placed a second cup under the drip. He poured a cup and replaced the pot under the drip to finish brewing.

"Sorry, Bob," said Bill, "this spry old gent."

"Bob is my friend," said Shania.

"Baby, please. Not yet," said Bill.

Shania looked at her watch. Bob brought two more cups of coffee to the table, and they all sat down.

"You can stow your weapon, Bob," said Bill. "I don't reckon we'll be gunfighting."

Bob holstered the pistol and stashed it in a kitchen drawer.

"Well?" said Shania.

"Babe," said Bill.

"No starting with 'Babe,' no terms of endearment. Just talk," she said.

"Okay," said Bill. "Any more dictums? Rules of engagement? I admit the thought of you with somebody else, even Bob here, brings out the brute in me, even though I understand it's a paternal thing between you two. It is paternal, right? Or platonic. Bob, don't tell me you're smitten. I knew it. I've got two words for you. Old man. Get serious."

"That's four," said Bob.

Bill turned to Shania, "Babe, if you don't love me, I'll live through it. But I can't keep chasing after you. It's not going to stay like that with me. If all you want is to keep it casual, just say so."

"I want to keep it casual," said Shania.

"Fine," said Bill, "let's just talk about the case."

"Oh, it's a case now, is it?" said Shania.

"Bob," said Bill, "what is the extent of the surveillance at the Lodge?"

"What surveillance?"

"That's what Marshal Berne Ventine said. He wants you to call him, by the way. So get over yourself. Don't be so recalcitrant with your intel."

"Recalcitrant?" Bob cut his eyes at Shania. She gave him back a look.

"It's a word," said Bill. He leaned back in the chair and looked at Shania and Bob. "So, what have y'all been up to?"

Shania said, "How do we know we're not being bugged right now?"

Bob said, "We don't."

"He wouldn't do you like that, would he?" said Shania. "Your Marshal friend?"

"Fifty-fifty chance," said Bob.

"How can you live like that?"

"It's not a problem until people come over," said Bob, "visitors who insist on talking."

"Your Marshal friend about had a conniption when I arrested Mikhail," said Bill. "What's that tell you? Who else is undercover at the Lodge?"

"It doesn't pay to antagonize the Marshals Service," said Bob.

"He antagonized me first. This is my town," said Bill. "He doesn't keep me out of the loop. I keep him out of the loop."

"Boys," said Shania, "we're getting nowhere."

"I need something to eat," said Bill. "Bob, you got any eggs?"

Shania slapped her palm on the table. "What does Ari Wilkes want? What is that shitbag doing here?"

"Spending government money," said Bill. "Your tax dollars. He's not really rich. He's just a pimp. He had a little network in Alabama. He's not connected down here."

Shania envisioned Constance Featherton, sole heir to the Featherton fortune, rebuffing unwanted advances from the pimp, Wilkes, whose obvious plan was to lay claim to everything she owned and everything she would ever inherit.

"It's none of our affair," said Bill. "We need to back off. That's what Marshal Ventine advises. We stay out of it and let them do their jobs."

As he spoke, Bill rolled his eyes up and swiveled his head from side to side.

"Constance knew Ari when they were kids," said Shania. "They were engaged. She canceled the wedding. There's a deep grudge between them that won't stay buried."

"If Constance opened up to you about that, she had a reason," said Bob.

"She's scared," said Shania. "Ari shows up as a guest, pitches woo. She tells him to fuck off. He laughs at her. He can't believe she still holds a grudge against him."

Bill said, "What did he do to her? Back then."

"She didn't go into details," said Shania.

CHAPTER TWENTY-FIVE
THE DARK TUNNEL

Shania and Billy left together to go out for breakfast at Shelton's Big Boy Buffet. Bob declined their invitation to graze with them. He could stomach maybe a crust of bread, not the grease feast waiting under the sneeze shield at Shelton's. As the confrontational phase of their morning grew more affectionate, Bob missed the bickering.

Shania had the gall to give Bob a peck on the cheek as she left, as if he'd been no more than her avuncular pal all along. At least he had the place to himself again for a while.

They had promised to return. He had friends now who dropped by at all hours.

Bob dressed for work and ate a piece of toast.

The sharp knock on the door was Berne Ventine.

"Long time, no see," said Bob, opening the door wide.

"Bob, how about a cup of your famous java?"

Berne followed him back into the kitchen where Bob poured a cup of the lukewarm dregs and put it in the microwave. He punched the beverage button, pre-set for thirty seconds.

"You're probably wondering why I'm here," said Berne.

"No," said Bob, "more like, how long you plan to stay. Some of us have to go to work."

"I won't keep you, Bob," he said. "I owe you an apology, and, as you know, the Marshals Service does not apologize. So, when I say I'm sorry, Bob, I only bugged your apartment because I had to, it's me apologizing, not the Marshals Service."

"I'll be lodging a formal complaint," said Bob, "in the form of a strongly worded letter."

"Good. That's all there is to it, then. Now give me the book," said Berne.

"Berne," said Bob, "as explanations go, that one's unsat."

The microwave dinged. Berne took the cup out, swirled the coffee around. He tasted it and gulped it down.

"You'll be late for work," he said.

"The short version will do," said Bob. "Come on. You've been holding out on me."

"While you're bumbling around in the dark tunnel with your new best friends," said Berne.

"Money laundering," said Bob. "Raleigh Featherton was a money launderer."

"Well, now," said Berne. "You kept that little secret. Not sharing with the triumvirate? The triangulators?"

"Took me long enough to figure it out," said Bob.

"Billions of dollars in constant transit through East-West Entertainment Group, parent company of one of the last and largest traveling carnivals. That's just one ledger. With eighteen more, do the math," said Berne.

"You do the math," said Bob.

"Wilhoite pitched the idea to the Bureau," said Berne. "He would hand them complete control of the Featherton money laundering franchise. Guaranteed delivery of the ledgers.

"The Bureau sold us his hopeful tale, of a death blow dealt from within hard enough to decimate the Dixie Mafia.

"As Wilkes, Aronoyad would rekindle his old romance with Constance, from whom as a young lad, he was separated by tragic circumstance. He knew her as no one did and promised his influence would secure for us her complete cooperation. She would name him CEO of East-West Entertainment Group, parent company of one of the last and largest traveling carnivals, and business would continue with barely a blip. He would run it for us, and we would soon know everything there was to know about the DM's money."

"You couldn't just ask her to cooperate?" said Bob.

"Too risky," said Berne. "You can't give people room to refuse when the stakes are this high. Or they will refuse, and then where are you?"

Bob looked at Berne without saying anything.

"May I remind you that this was not my plan," said Berne.

"Whose plan was it?" said Bob.

"The feds have the deep pockets," said Berne. "You don't want to meet those troglodytes. They are so embarrassed now that their boy is showing his true colors, running skeeze and burgling guests, they're about to bail and leave me holding this big stank diaper. After we come to find out Ms. Constance despises Wilkes to the nth degree. His ya-ya influence with her is nil, so no, no progress on that front, sorry. Now Ari wants to be an hotelier."

"You created an evil genie," said Bob.

"We did," said Berne. "And we'll uncreate him."

"He doesn't seem worried about that," said Bob.

"Give me the book, now."

"I'm still reading it," said Bob.

Berne's brow furrowed. His voice lowered. "You have a translation?"

"Berne, the Senator's name is in it."

"So?"

"Is your name in it?"

Berne took a step back. He put his hand over his heart.

"Oh, now that is hurtful, Bob," he said.

"It would explain a lot," said Bob.

"You cut me to the quick, my friend."

The tremolo in Berne's tone sounded theatrical, uber sardonic, like the voice of an evil wizard in a Balkan puppet show.

Bob said, "Don't protest so much."

Berne's voice changed to sincerity mode. Without affectation, he said, "Bob, I live in a shack. And sometimes in a van down by the river. I've got nothing but my honor in this job. For you to impugn me like that, you, Bob, the one wit I admire, yeah, you, Bob; you wound me."

"So your name is in it," said Bob.

"If it is or isn't," said Berne, "is not the point. The point is you believe it might be. I deserve better from you, Bob. I thought we were tight. Oh, well. So long, podnah. Now get me the damn book, and the codex. Right now, Bob. How many copies are there?"

Berne's gun was out, his patience on the wane.

Bob said, "Now you pull a gun on me in my own house. I don't like that."

Bob moved within reach of the kitchen drawer where his pistol was stashed. He was not eager for their little tiff to escalate. It was not like he didn't have a choice. He could give Berne the Necronomicon and its codex and be done with it. Or not. Not felt better.

"Bob, stay away from those kitchen drawers," said Berne. "What are you looking for, a spoon? Come on. Don't make this ugly."

"I was looking for a first aid kit."

"Bob," said Berne, "I'm not going to shoot you."

"You can't force me legally to give you the book, can you?"

"Actually, I can, but I won't. The book is yours. Call me if you ever have a problem, okay? I might be able to help you out of a jam someday. You know, maybe."

"Alright," said Bob. "You can have the Necronomicon. I'll keep the codex."

"No, the hell you will. How much has the reporter read?"

"Enough to know there's a lot more."

Berne leered at him, "I swear, Bob, it sounded like you were getting somewhere before that farm boy showed up."

Bob ignored the jibe.

"Bob, tell me you didn't give farm boy the ledger."

"It's in a safe place," said Bob. "After work. I'll have it then."

"Bob, you're lying. It's in your room," said Berne.

Bob made a grand sweep of one outstretched arm. "Be my guest," he said.

"Bob, by tomorrow, East Bunkie, Wyoming, might look pretty sweet to you."

"I'm not going to Bunkie," said Bob.

"Just give me the damn book," said Berne.

"It's not here. Turn the place upside down. Have at it. Let yourself out and lock up when you leave," said Bob.

Berne followed Bob to the door. He came outside with him and trailed him to his truck.

Bob unlocked his truck and climbed in behind the wheel. Berne lingered by the open driver door, blocking it from closing. "You kept it in here," he said, pointing to the torn manila package on the passenger side floorboard.

"That's something else," said Bob.

"Bob, quit screwing around. You can't keep the codex."

"All right," said Bob. He picked up the package from the floorboard and held it like a baby to his chest with his left arm half extended to ward off Berne. "My receipt," he said.

Berne whipped out a little notebook and scribbled a note and his signature. He tore it off the pad and handed it over in exchange for the package. Berne had to tug it out of his hands. He slid the black leather bound ledger out of the envelope and riffled through its pages.

Bob read the receipt out loud: "Received one ledger from Bob Day. Berne Ventine B.V."

"B. V.?"

"Bon Voyage," Berne backed away from Bob's truck.

Bob tried to hand him back the receipt. He said, "Write down 'And one codex."

"No," said Berne, walking away. "There is no codex."

CHAPTER TWENTY-SIX
QUALIFIERS

Duncan Upton preferred to schedule important meetings early in the day. At eighty-five, he was at his vigorous best in the morning. He rose early every day; worked out for a half hour in his home gym, showered, shaved, ate a light breakfast, and was ready to conduct business by eight or eight-thirty. As owner of the Lodge, it was his prerogative to call the tune; others could dance to it or not at their peril.

He arrived at the Lodge in a car driven by his lawyer, Godfrey Daniels, and was met at the front doors at precisely eight forty-five by Mr. Yelvington and his lawyer, Ms. Thelmarie Drummond. Her hair was platinum white, and her skin was as smooth as an egg. She wore a twill bespoke suit and a taupe silk blouse, and some kind of orthopedic shoes.

"Good morning, Ms. Drummond," said Duncan Upton, offering his hand. He knew his canyon gray hairpiece was on straight because he had last checked it in the car and had not touched or bumped it since. That knowledge stood him in good stead and added to his charm.

"I hope you weren't inconvenienced coming out here so early," he smiled, showing perfect teeth.

"I'm pleased to be here," said Ms. Drummond. "Such a lovely place."

After handshakes all around, Mr. Upton said, "Shall we?"

Just Don held the door wide open for them and escorted the party to the lobby elevator. The elevator went up one floor and opened on the mezzanine outside the Innlet Restaurant and Bar. They followed Renaldo to a private table in the Ocean Room South, a small meeting room with tall, arched windows overlooking the ocean.

Beige linen covered the conference table set for four with water goblets, notepads, pens, and pitchers of ice water. A white linen napkin covered a basket of hot scones, biscotti and croissants on a sideboard with a silver coffee service and silver carafes of orange juice, grapefruit juice and tea.

The four took their seats and allowed Renaldo to provide service and withdraw.

When all were ready, Godfrey Daniels cleared his throat and spoke.

"This meeting is called by the minority owner, Mr. Yelvington, for the purpose of the disposition, in the manner of his choice, of the balance of his interest in the Belle Rive Lodge and Club. As stated in prior meetings, the majority shareholder, Mr. Duncan Upton, raises no objections and places no restrictions on Mr. Yelvington's intentions as described, nor claims any right whatsoever to interfere with Mr. Yelvington's directions. With that on record, Ms. Drummond, it's your meeting."

"Thank you, Mr. Daniels," said Ms. Drummond. "Mr. Yelvington wishes to dispose of his entire remaining interest in the Lodge and Club in the following manner: By private auction, to which qualified management personnel have been invited.

"Bidding will open at two hundred fifty thousand dollars for the block of five shares. Management personnel were given thirty-six hours to qualify, a strategy designed to discourage tentative applications. We have three qualified parties: David Moriarty, General Manager, Constance Featherton, Front Desk Supervisor, and Diana Bytheway, Membership Director. We propose that this private auction proceed as planned."

"Be it resolved that I voice no objection," said Duncan Upton.

"Be it also resolved," said Ms. Drummond, "that partnerships, confederations or joint ownerships of any kind shall not be validated, nor will attempts to purchase said block of shares by proxy. The purpose of this sale is to facilitate the continuation of a single, responsible, minority owner of shares in the Lodge and Club."

"Be it so stipulated," said Mr. Daniels. "However, any overtures initiated by the new owner on some future date, for instance, shall not be bound by the stipulation, nor shall any transaction resulting thereof be construed as a violation of said stipulation."

Ms. Drummond turned to Mr. Yelvington. "Do you understand the point Mr. Daniels makes?"

"Yes," said Mr. Yelvington. "Should the new owner choose to initiate the sale of his or her own shares to Mr. Duncan Upton, or to anyone else, it shall be his right, or hers, to do so, as he or she sees fit. Nothing I can do about that."

"Be it resolved that Mr. Yelvington agrees to the terms as expressed."

"Let's do it," said Mr. Upton.

"This auction was scheduled for eleven o'clock," said Ms. Drummond. "Preparations have been made."

"I don't have all day to fool around," said Mr. Upton to Mr. Daniels. "Let's see if we can't move it up." He glanced at his watch, a thin, elegant Philippe Patek. "Let's say ten."

"I'll call around," said Mr. Daniels. He stood up and left the room.

Mr. Upton beamed a great wide rictus of a smile across the table at Mr. Yelvington.

"Well, Shadrach," he said, "you led me a merry chase."

"It's been fun," said Mr. Yelvington.

"You're going to miss me," said Mr. Upton.

"Not as much as you might think," said Mr. Yelvington.

Mr. Upton laughed. "Well, I'll miss you, Shad."

"I know you will," said Mr. Yelvington.

"What do you think of your prospects?"

"I think I may have made a mistake," said Mr. Yelvington.

"It's not too late to cancel."

"No," said Mr. Yelvington. "We'll roll with it."

Mr. Daniels returned, clicking his phone shut.

"Done," he said. "Auction's at ten."

"This meeting is adjourned," said Ms. Drummond.

Duncan Upton stood and shook Ms. Drummond's hand again.

"A pleasure, Ms. Drummond. Shad. We'll see you in about an hour."

"You may as well hang around," said Mr. Yelvington. "Where you running off to?"

"Walk about." Duncan Upton set off at a brisk pace toward the restroom.

•   •   •

Dick Skinner knocked lightly on Constance's office door before he poked his head in. "Got a minute?" he asked.

She waved him in. "Sure."

Dick took the chair across the desk from her. He tugged on a too tight collar with one finger. "So," he said, "how's it feel not to need this job anymore?"

"I never needed it," said Constance, "not in the way you might think."

"Well, it makes it kind of awkward now between us. You could have told me."

"Why?"

"Well, you might have considered that, as your lover, I might want to know that you're worth, what, a billion dollars?"

"You're not my lover," said Constance. "You're just my boss."

Dick's hand reflexively touched his groin. "Well, you're not technically a manager," he said, "so how'd you qualify?"

"I completed management training," she said. "Technically, I am in management."

"If you outbid David he'll fire you," said Dick.

"Not if I'm his boss," said Constance.

"He'd rather work things out with you."

"I bet he would," said Constance.

"He wants those shares," said Dick.

"So do I."

"Don't make me tell him no, Con." A desperate note in his voice quavered.

Her amusement glazed over. She picked up a stack of comment cards, tapped them straight and set them back down on her desk.

"We all do things we don't want to do, sometimes," she said.

•   •   •   •   •

Diana Bytheway was not in her office when David went looking for her. As Membership Director, she kept her own hours. Lately that included room service breakfasts with Ari in his suite. What she did on her own time was no one's business.

She looked across the wide hotel bed at Ari on the patio in his robe. He was gazing out to sea. "Please, God," she wanted to scream, "let this man love me!"

Instead, she gathered her clothes and dressed.

He had broken down every internal barrier she had, dissolved years of inhibitions and psychoses. He had washed them away like they never were and left her ravaged, panting, sated, craven, prostrate, ass up on all fours, begging for more debasement, free, at last, to be a man's pet whore without shame. She understood that it was never love with Ari, and that it never would or could be love again. She had known for a few days already that that part of him was gone.

Ari was counting on her to clinch the deal.

So was David.

Ari claimed to represent Constance, but the thought of Ari with That Bitch was like swallowing a stone. Every time Diana imagined them together was like swallowing another stone.

Ari had told her the story of their early love and courtship. Diana had barely endured it; his immigrant boy story, how he had met an old man on a park bench in Tampa who talked to him about the wide world and gave him a job and a home with his traveling carnival. He had met Constance when she was sixteen and working the midway with a knife thrower. Ari got her pregnant. They were going to be married, and Ari would have become an instant citizen. She blamed him when she lost the baby and tried to break his heart. Twenty-some years later, her name was still like honey on his lips.

Diana would suffer any number of other women for Ari, but to see the one enshrined in his heart as other than an enemy was too hard. How could she not hate That Bitch?

Ari wanted her to work the auction with Constance against David. "Don't worry about your job," he told her, "David won't be here much longer."

Easy for him to say.

Diana had known David Moriarty for many years. She considered David a dear friend, and up until a few days ago, she would never have imagined herself betraying his trust for any reason. Now everything in her life had changed. Her mind and body were under Ari's hand when she was with him, and, though it felt like doom to obey him, it was the perverse thrill of that doomed feeling that she loved the most about being near him. When she was away from him his power over her felt even greater. Her whole body ached to return to him.

Ari stood on the patio balcony, watching Claudia jog down the beach. He waved to her and opened his robe as she looked up. Claudia smiled up at him and kept running.

Diana checked a text on her phone and stood up. She opened the patio door. "I have to go," she said. "The time slot's been moved up to ten."

"What? Who moved it?" said Ari.

"Mr. Upton. I guess he wants to get it over with."

"Danitshka, you sell to me, not him."

"I know," she said.

"No mistake. I kill you."

Diana smiled, "You kill me."

.   .   .

"Fifty to Maintenance."

Bob unclipped the radio from his belt and answered, "Go ahead Fifty."

Constance asked, "Bob, can you please meet me at the front desk?"

"I can meet you by the pergola," said Bob. "I'm there now. That's the area commonly known as the trellis area."

"Fine," said Constance. She left her office and the front desk area and slipped out the side door to the area known to all employees and members as the trellis area, which would never be called the pergola area, except by Bob, even if it was a pergola rather than a trellis. Bob was so ridiculous.

He was adjusting the foot pump hose by the south ramp to the beach where a short length of hose was used to wash beach sand off feet, shoes, kids and pets. Constance squinted at him in the bright morning sun.

"Sorry to sound cryptic," said Bob. "Your office is probably bugged."

"What?"

"This whole hotel is bugged, although, maybe not out here. What did you want?"

"What?"

"You wanted to see me?"

"Oh, Bob," she sighed. It had come to this, to placing her trust in Bob. "Can you put me in touch with, you know, someone who can protect me from Ari?"

Bob took a moment to gauge her sincerity. It was a moment to savor, but no pleasure came with it. "I can do that," he said.

"Not you, Bob. I meant, you know."

"I know what you meant," said Bob.

"Can you call him now?"

"Right now?"

"Yes, Bob. Right now."

She had her cell out already and handed it over. He punched in a number.

"You'll want to get a new phone," he said, "and never use this phone again."

"What?"

Bob held up his palm to shush her.

"Berne," said Bob, into the phone, "You're going to want the Cone of Silence."

He handed the phone back to her. "Is there anything else I can do for you today?"

David met Duncan Upton midway up on the lobby stairs.

"Hello, Duncan," said David.

"David," said Duncan. "A word?"

They paused on the landing where the staircase turned and stood by the window near the potted palm where several listening devices were hidden. Duncan Upton often spoke softly so that people would listen more closely to him. That technique worked. David cocked his good ear toward Mr. Upton and listened with all his might.

"Regardless how this charade pans out, David, I want you to know that I consider your stewardship here at the Lodge exemplary."

"Thank you, sir," said David.

"No brag, just fact."

David nodded. "Guns of Will Sonnett," he said, "best TV western of all time."

Duncan Upton smiled from his soul at the young man sharing a golden television memory with him. "Damn right. Old Walter Brennan."

"They don't make them like that anymore," said David.

"No, sir," said Duncan Upton, "No sir, they do not."

They shook hands warmly, bonded over the best western series in television history, and continued on their separate ways, Duncan down the staircase, David up.

At the top, David said hello to Buddy, the maitre'd.

"Good luck today, David," said Buddy.

"Thanks. Buddy, do we know who's running the auction? What company?"

"I'm not quite sure," said Buddy. "I think it has red in it, red hat, red dot, something like that."

"Red Door?"

"Maybe. I really don't know."

David said, "Think, Buddy, is it Red Door, or not?"

Buddy said, "Travis would know. He set the room up."

"Well, Buddy, do you know where Travis is?" David asked.

"No, sir. I do not know," said Buddy. "He was just here a moment ago."

David did an about face and headed for the restroom. The upstairs lobby bathrooms serving the restaurant and lounge were the largest and the nicest in the hotel, with marble floors and walls and granite countertops, very substantial.

David entered one of two stalls and closed the door. He unscrewed the cap on the vial of coke and tapped out a fair sized bump on the back of his hand. He bent over it quickly with a short straw in his nostril and whiffed it up, leaving no trace, and put the straw away. The toilet flushed automatically. He opened the stall door and went over to the sink. As he washed his hands, Duncan Upton came in.

"Who's running the auction?" David asked.

"Red Hat, out of Atlanta, I believe," said Mr. Upton. "They've been around a long time."

"Okay, then," said David. "Not Red Door?"

"Wait now, let me think," said Mr. Upton. "Red Door? I don't know. I can't remember. It had red in it."

"Maybe I'll ask Shad if he knows," said David.

"I wouldn't," said Upton. "Best to fall back now and just play it as it lies."

"Alright, then," said David. He dried his hands with a fine paper napkin imprinted with the Lodge Shell logo as Duncan Upton washed his hands in the sink beside him, both of them facing a big mirror. The wastebasket was situated on Upton's far side, next to his right knee. To toss his napkin, David would have to walk around behind him. In his hypersensitive, energized state, that felt to David like it held the potential of possibly appearing awkward, so David kept drying his hands with the napkin, waiting for Duncan to finish and move, while Duncan dried his own hands with a napkin and took his sweet time about it. He seemed to be making a mental tally of every age spot and wrinkle on his face.

Finally, David left with the damp napkin balled up in his fist. He made a mental note to have a second wastebasket placed in the Innlet bathrooms as soon as possible.

CHAPTER TWENTY-SEVEN
FOR THE GREATER GLORY OF THE LODGE

In the maintenance shop, Karl overloaded his paint cart with tools and equipment for one of his most dreadful missions, the painting of the outside concrete steps and landing with xylene-based silicone acrylic concrete stain. In addition to the noxious product sloshing in a half full metal five gallon bucket, he packed a respirator, heavy gloves, a roller and brush setup, a roller stick, three orange safety cones, a roll of yellow CAUTION tape, wet paint signs and a broom and dustpan onto his rolling cart. With these items piled and tenuously balanced on his cart, he set out through the garage toward the stairwell steps.

He met Bob at the midpoint of the garage walking back toward the shop with a light bulb in his hand.

"Look on my works, ye mighty, and despair," said Karl.

"Nam Maior Laus Tabernus," said Bob.

They passed each other with *esprit de corps.*

For the Greater Glory of the Lodge was the motto he and Bob had come up with and boldly translated into Latin. In times of stress and great tedium having a Latin motto to bandy about was a definite plus. Karl wanted to see the motto imprinted below the shell on all Lodge logos, but so far, its existence was known only to Bob and Karl.

"Nam Maior Laus Tabernus," Karl repeated the motto several times in sonorous, pontifical tones, testing the dead resonance of the parking garage.

The stairwell to be painted was a favored means of egress for departures. At the southern end of the walkways to the rooms on the boulevard side, it provided the closest access to the bell stand and the front desk.

In order to paint the lower section from the landing on the first level down to the landing on the ground floor level, cones and caution tape and wet paint signs needed to be placed in at least three locations to divert guests to alternate routes. The actual painting took less than half an hour, usually, but the setting up and the sweeping and the prep often took longer.

When Karl worked with the xylene-based stain, also known as liquid cancer, the respirator and gloves were his first and last defense against the most toxic solvent in the paint world. He worked as fast as possible to get it over with. Absorbed through the skin or lungs, xylene entered the body and stayed forever. Unlike common solvents, it was non-fat-soluble; it collected in fat cells and did not break down over time. It formed pockets of black potential death in fat cells and remained in the body mutating cells and exacerbating any number of problematic issues like cancer, nerve damage and dementia.

The fumes of xylene based silicone acrylic stain were so strong in a closed space like a corridor or a stairwell that no one coming near could fail to note that serious painting was underway, yet it was a common occurrence for members or guests to ignore all barriers and wet paint signs put up for their benefit and ask Karl, even while his face was covered with a respirator, even while the roller stick in his hands was spreading paint across the floor, if the paint was still wet and if it would be okay for them to walk across the freshly painted floor.

The xylene based paint dried extremely fast but never fast enough. There was always someone oblivious to the signs, the tape, the cones, and even the fumes. It was maddening.

By the time, Karl had reached the bottom step of the stair and painted the landing, and the final three steps to the cobblestone walkway outside the front of the building, the paint at the top of the first landing was dry enough to sustain foot traffic. The paint on the top few steps might even be dry or close to dry. But at the bottom of the steps, the paint was not yet dry enough to walk on. It needed maybe four more minutes.

Upon finishing, Karl tore off his respirator and stepped away from the site to breathe fresh air. Despite all the signs, it was his custom to stay in the area and wait for the paint to dry, to protect his work.

He had just turned his head away for a moment when he heard a cry from an elderly woman standing on the last bottom step of the stair. Thin and ancient, dressed in a lime green pantsuit with matching lime green shoes, she had stepped past the cone on the landing above and

146

paid no notice to the deadly fumes while proceeding down the stairs. Three-quarters of the way down the stairs, she had encountered wet paint underfoot. At the same time, the fumes had begun to affect her, and her motor functions slowed. She stood on the bottom step calling out as the fast drying paint fused the soles of her shoes to the steps.

"I'm sorry," she said, "I saw those wet paint signs, I thought they meant the walls were wet. I didn't touch the walls."

"No, ma'am," said Karl, "it's the steps, and the deck."

"Oh, dear," she said. When she tried to lift one foot, she nearly lost her balance and fell forward. Both her shoes were stuck to the stairs. She struggled to lift one foot then the other until she ripped her right shoe free of the paint and stepped her right foot onto the next step up. Then she pulled her left foot free of her shoe, which remained stuck to the bottom step.

The landing was still too wet for Karl to walk across to help her. He watched her, worried that she would faint from the fumes and sprawl headlong onto the wet deck with her feet still attached to the steps by her shoes. She leaned on the railing and carefully slid her left foot back into her shoe. With a tug, she yanked it free. Beige xylene paint stuck to the soles and stained the lime green of her shoes and also the hem of her pantsuit.

She muttered, "Oh, dear, oh, dear," as she retreated back up the steps.

Karl watched her go, knowing her shoes and pants were ruined, knowing that she would feel horrible for the rest of the day from the fumes. She was in the thick of it. Another minute or two and she would have passed right out on the stairwell. She was already half stupefied. Karl knew also that he was at fault for setting up a mere three cones instead of four. But it was hard enough carrying three cones on his cart. He was just trying not to make two trips. Although he had placed a cone on the landing above the first level, he had neglected to place a cone at the top of the stairs; also he had negligently failed to block off with tape either the top or the bottom of the stairway from the upper to the lower walkway. The old woman had blithely walked down the stairs past one cone and one wet paint sign, unimpeded by either warning.

Within minutes, the paint on the landing was dry, and Karl walked across it to touch up the steps. He wished he had a camera to capture the image of her two shoe prints on the bottom step. He used both the brush and the roller to touch up the steps, destroying the evidence, making it look like it never happened.

John Thomas arrived with a yellow covered manual, *How to Conduct an Auction for Dummies*, concealed among his other equipment. He wasn't busy that day, and when asked on short notice to conduct the auction, he had jumped at the chance. He had done a little research and was up for the challenge. He intended to forego the traditional auctioneer's chant, which took years to master, he had heard, and so it seemed.

As eager as he was to learn the auctioneer's patois, the Lodge was not the best venue for practice. He decided to keep it simple and do it his way.

John Thomas set up his equipment in the Ocean Room East near the podium. His digital video projector flashed a slideshow of images onto a screen, exterior landscape shots of the Lodge from all angles, including aerial. Many of the shots were old. The building had not changed a great deal, but the dunes in front of it had shrunk, and the surrounding lots to the south and west had been developed. North Florida's scruffy scrub oak dunes had given way to a row of luxury condos. Homeowners had kept the high rises off this stretch of coastline, but across the street, west of the boulevard, height code restrictions were not as stringent and a four-story condo building, The Cloisters, had risen.

The slideshow documented the Lodge in all its stages, from construction over pristine sand dunes on through several renovations. Smiling faces of employees through the years held together like a tapestry a fluid mélange of time travel and nostalgia, reinforced with a steady parade of hard numbers. Statistically, the Lodge had averaged over a million dollars net profit every year for the past twelve years, since the time of the last major renovations. John Thomas did the math for everyone, demonstrating how a net profit of an even million a year earns the owner of five shares an annual check for fifty thousand dollars.

The room was arranged with spectator seating for non-participating managers on the right. On the left, the owners sat with their lawyers. In the middle, seated at three separate tables, the bidders watched the slideshow with rapt attention and listened to the commentary.

"There were some lean years," said John Thomas, "before the Lodge became a Four Diamond hotel. And these are lean years now, as we all know. But the Lodge continues to show significant net profits each year and remains a four diamond property, thanks to our intrepid staff and our extraordinary dedication to service, which is consistently rated at the five-diamond level.

"The opportunity offered to you today comes around maybe once in a lifetime if you're lucky, and you three bidders are here to see that deal go down. But first, a little story. I call this, the Story of the Lodge:

"Once upon a time, a builder built an oceanfront hotel. He was hired to build it. He didn't design it. He agreed to build it according to the blueprints drawn and approved by architects. But there were problems with the plans, and when the builder recognized these problems, he went to the original owners, the Swindell brothers, and showed them proof that the concrete foundation slab that had been poured across the sand dune was shifting at the expansion joint. That posed a problem that required immediate attention. The foundation slab needed additional support on the southern end.

"You fix it," said the owners to the builder. "You're the builder."

"It's your expense, not mine," the builder replied. "The slab satisfies the specs, but the south end is settling and needs to be shored up. That's an additional cost of a hundred, maybe two hundred grand, easy."

The Swindell brothers said, "We're over budget, as it is."

"I can't build on the slab until it's fixed," said the builder.

So they all sat down and examined their options, and what they came up with was an agreement by the builder to shore up the slab on his expense in exchange for five full shares in the Lodge and Club. The builder accepted the agreement. The Lodge was built and the builder, Mr. Shadrach Yelvington, assumed ownership of these five shares that have come to be known ever since as the Yelvington shares.

"The story doesn't end there. The Swindell brothers sold their interest in the Lodge and Club after eleven years, during which time, the Lodge consistently showed a net profit, but the numbers improved after the new owner, Mr. Duncan Upton, took over. At the time of his purchase of the Swindell brothers' shares in the Lodge, Mr. Upton offered to buy Mr. Yelvington's shares, as well, but Mr. Yelvington declined his offer. He held on to his five shares through thick and thin. Through good times and bad, he has been the living, breathing soul of the Lodge and Club since the first earth was turned on this project. And now, he is finally ready to pass on his legacy here at the Lodge, a tradition of caring, above all, about the quality of the work we do.

"The story of the Lodge is the story of the Yelvington shares. These are the shares you will bid on today. As owner of these shares, you will bear the burden of conscience, for you will become the new conscience of the Lodge. True, you may be outvoted by the majority owner, but your voice will always be heard at every Owners Meeting. The rest is up to you."

Duncan leaned over to whisper to Shad, "Didn't we agree to get Red Hat on this?"

"You agreed to let me handle it," said Shad.

"I was going to say," said Duncan. "They can't touch our boy when he's on. Every once in a while he reminds me why I keep him around."

John Thomas looked around the room, saw several eyes subtly wiped. He had their attention.

"And now, the moment is here," he said. "In this auction, we have up for bid one lot of five full shares in the Lodge and Club. One lot and three bidders. Opening bid is two hundred and fifty thousand dollars. Bids will be in increments of five. Two hundred and fifty thousand dollars, do I hear two five five?"

"Two sixty," said David.

"Two sixty, do I hear two six five, two six five, any minute now, two six five."

"Two sixty-five," said Constance. She looked over at David and flashed a smile.

He mouthed, "You're fired."

Constance's smile widened, as if she thought this was going to be fun.

"Two six five, need two seventy. Two seven oh, let's go. Two seventy, two seventy."

"Two-seventy," said Diana. She would not look at David, nor he at her.

"Two-eighty," said David.

"Two eighty. Two eight oh. Do I hear two eighty-five?"

"Two eighty-five," said Diana.

"Two eight five," said John Thomas, "two eighty-five."

"Two ninety," said Constance."

"Two ninety. Am I hearing two nine five? Give me two nine five, please, two nine five."

"Two ninety-five," said Diana.

David's desperation could not be measured in increments of five. He had allowed himself to hope for less resistance. Now he knew he was up against a wall of bigger money. Bigger than Upton's. Insofar as he knew Duncan Upton to be frugal, David knew he would not show his hand, yet Constance bid fearlessly. Where were these women getting their money? Was he paying them too much? Diana had come from money but was never one to flaunt it. And Constance, merely being an heiress didn't mean she had the money in her hands already, did it? Both those bitches had more money than he did. Either one could be a shill for Upton. David felt the shares slipping away, his once-in-a-lifetime opportunity to have and to hold a piece of The Lodge. He was about to start crying inside when he noticed Duncan Upton's reaction to Diana's last bid. Duncan raised a fist to his chin and kept it there, holding a pose like The Thinker with his elbow on his knee. It felt like a signal to David, one not directed to him.

"Two ninety-five, do I hear three hundred. Three hundred, three zero zero. Do I hear three? Two ninety-five, do I hear three? Three oh, oh, three hundred. Two ninety-five going once."

David's top-end figure was three ten. He couldn't go any deeper into the hole than that.

"Three hundred," said Constance.

"Three hundred, is it three oh five? Three oh five or three hundred. We have three hundred, three hundred, three hundred thousand dollars going once."

"Three-ten," said David.

"We have three ten, three hundred ten, do we have three fifteen? Three fifteen?"

David looked at Diana, willing her to look his way and see the earnest plea in his eyes. She kept her head down and shook it ever so slightly and closed her eyes.

"Three hundred ten thousand dollars going once," said John Thomas.

Constance smiled at David and said, "Three-fifteen."

"Three fifteen, ladies and gentlemen. Three fifteen. Do I hear three twenty?"

David was silent. The pencil he had wedged between his knuckles snapped, sounding as loud as a thunderclap. Constance kept smiling like the sun was shining. Diana bowed her head. She stole a look at Duncan Upton, still posed as The Thinker.

"Three fifteen, three fifteen, three hundred fifteen thousand dollars going once."

Duncan Upton held his pose.

"Three hundred fifteen hundred thousand dollars going twice."

Duncan Upton sat up straight in his chair.

"Three twenty," said Diana.

"Three twenty-five," said Constance.

"Three thirty," said Diana.

Constance laughed, "This is fun. Three thirty-five."

Duncan Upton resumed his Rodinesque posture.

"Three-thirty-five," said John Thomas, "three hundred thirty-five, do I hear three hundred forty? Three hundred forty, any minute now, three hundred forty. We have three hundred thirty-five, three hundred thirty-five hundred thousand dollars going once."

Diana covered her face with her hands. She was done.

"Three hundred thirty thousand dollars going twice."

Duncan Upton held his pose.

"Three hundred thirty thousand dollars going three times and we have sold the Yelvington shares, folks, to Ms. Constance Featherton."

David reached across to be the first to congratulate her, but his fury was evident as he exited the Ocean Room. He encountered Mikhail malingering in the hallway outside the door to the Wine Room. "You're fired," he said.

He stormed into the kitchen through the Room Service doors and looked around like he was looking for someone else to fire. All the kitchen workers appeared to be engaged in fruitful labor, so he kept on through the kitchen and passed into the bar area through the kitchen door. Renaldo was standing by the bar watching a silent soccer game on the television over the bar.

David came up behind him and tapped him on the shoulder. "You're fired," he said.

He went on past Buddy's podium to the Innlet restroom. Buddy had the grace to be absent from his post at that moment. In the restroom, David tapped out the rest of the coke on the granite countertop and snorted it sloppily. As the burn freeze rocketed to his brain he checked his appearance in the mirror. He still looked good. He wiped bits of white residue from his nostrils with a napkin and tossed it in the wastebasket.

He muttered under his breath, "Fucking motherfuckers."

He charged out of the bathroom and down the stairs at a fast clip.

At the Front Desk, Naila was pacifying an irate guest. She caught David's eye and beckoned to him to come to her aid.

"Mrs. Dunwoodie," said Naila, as David came up, "may I please introduce you to David Moriarty, our General Manager. Mr. Moriarty, this is Mrs. Dunwoodie, our guest. She's not feeling well."

"Hello, Mrs. Dunwoodie," said David. "How may I be of assistance to you today?"

"Well, my shoes are ruined," she said, "and I feel terrible. I think I may have been exposed to toxic vapors."

"My goodness," said David, "here at the Lodge?"

"I was coming down the stairs," she said, "and breathing the most awful smell. Then I was standing in wet paint. I nearly fainted, and now I have such a headache I may have to go to the emergency room."

"I am so sorry, Mrs. Dunwoodie," said David. "Were there no barriers set up, no wet paint signs?"

"I don't know if there were or not."

"Shall we call an ambulance for you, Mrs. Dunwoodie?"

"Oh, no, no, that's not necessary. I might be alright. I thought you should know."

"Thank you for telling me," said David. "I will see to it personally that that never happens again."

"And her shoes," said Naila, "and her pants."

David nodded to Naila. "Please see that her things are sent out for dry cleaning."

"Of course," said Naila. "And if we can't get the stains out, we'll go shopping."

"Yes, indeed," said David.

"I loved those shoes," said Mrs. Dunwoodie.

"Is there anything else I can do for you, today, Mrs. Dunwoodie?" David asked.

"No, you've been quite kind, thank you."

David nodded to Naila. "And Karl is where now?"

"Maybe the Maintenance shop? Should I call?"

"No," said David. "I'll find him."

CHAPTER TWENTY-EIGHT
AFTERMATH

Adjacent to the Ocean Room was the Wine Room, accessible through a pair of narrow wooden swinging doors studded with stately dadoes and finished to match the same olive green tones of the original pickling stain on the wainscot. The Wine Room featured a large wine cabinet with glass walls in both rooms. Through the shadowed double lenses of the half-filled cabinet, Ari had watched the auction in the Ocean Room from the cool dark privacy of the Wine Room.

He had seen Diana's glance pass over the cabinet and the turn of her head and the shift of her hips in her chair as she turned away, as if she had glimpsed a reflected image of his face in the darkened glass. She had known Ari was watching her and still she had betrayed him. Not that it was easy for her. She went for Upton's money. And the money let her down.

Ari didn't blame her. She had recognized him as the poor boy at the party, not in the same league with the gentleman billionaires.

All he had asked of her was to outbid Constance. That she did not do. The gambit with Upton proved her falsity. Now she was a prisoner of her own conscience.

And the real work with Constance could begin.

When David stormed out of the Ocean Room, Ari stood back from the glass of the wine cabinet wall into the dark of the Wine Room. He had no time to warn Mikhail. Mown down by David's rage, Mikhail stepped into the Wine Room after David had passed on.

Mikhail said, "David fired me."

"You deserved it," said Ari, "lurking in the hall. That is not five-diamond."

"You joke, cousin, ha-ha," said Mikhail, "but I'm the one fired."

"Be calm," said Ari. "Nothing warrants loss of composure."

Mikhail said, "You cannot defeat them all, Ari. They are a line up against you."

"Have no fear," said Ari. "If all else fails, we go to Canada."

As Ari watched from the Wine Room, the spectators departed. Constance and Diana exchanged pleasantries with the lawyers and the owners. They gave each other distant hugs. Diana did not linger. She shook Mr. Upton's hand, and a small shrug passed between them.

Ari's plan proceeded with him standing in the hall outside the Ocean Room as Constance came out on the heels of the Upton and the Yelvington parties. Ari used Mikhail to interrupt Constance's stride and to separate her from the others. As he stepped up and touched her elbow, she recoiled at his touch and backed away from his open hands.

"Connie, my love," he said. "Where do all the flowers go? All the years gone by. Only yesterday, we were children playing by the sea."

"You were never a child, Ari," said Constance.

Ari pressed a finger to his lips and shushed. "It is our destiny to work together. You know it's true. Now more than ever. Come, we must talk."

"No, not now," she said, but she followed him anyway down the corridor and out the connecting door to the stairs. They walked together without speaking, and she fell in line behind him down the stairs to the fountain courtyard and down the steps to the north beach ramp until they were both standing at the far end of the walkway over the dunes, leaning on the weathered railing, closer to the ocean than to dry land.

"There are no microphones here, except yours and mine," said Ari. "Here is mine." Ari showed her a tiny wafer no larger than a dime. He threw it into the sand.

Constance said, "I'm not wearing a recording device. Say what you have to say."

Ari looked around. "Do you feel safe here with me now?"

"Safe? No," she said. "Not at all."

"I am your protector," said Ari. "Con, you must distance yourself from East-West Entertainment Group. Make me CEO. Then you will be safe from all prosecution. Your money will be safe. Only then. The task force will not touch you. I will handle them."

"With my cooperation, they don't need you anymore," said Constance.

"You are wrong. Of course, they need me, and so do you, because you are not a criminal. How can you run a criminal organization when you are not a criminal?"

"I can run it," said Constance.

"But you can't run a five-diamond hotel at the same time," said Ari.

"The Lodge is still a four-diamond hotel," Constance reminded him, "for now. And I'm not running it. Yet."

"But you want to."

"Yes, I do," she admitted.

"As did I, for one day," said Ari. "But it's best for all concerned that cooler heads than mine run the hotel business."

"What makes you think your head would be any cooler as CEO of East-West?"

"Trust me," said Ari. "The hotel business is far more stressful than crime."

Constance said, "East-West Entertainment Group is a legitimate corporation."

"A legitimate criminal corporation," said Ari.

"Well, dream on about that trust thing," said Constance.

"Connie," said Ari, "Connie, Connie, Connie. Please don't tell me to dream on." He reached for her as she backed away. "Say anything but that, please. It is most annoying."

"Ari," said Constance, "let me tell you one thing."

Constance could dredge up no pity for him, no feeling other than loathing. She had hated him for far too long to be swayed by his charisma.

"East-West means nothing to me. That was Uncle Raleigh's world, not mine. They say he was worth billions, but it's all illegal. I can't let any of that touch me."

"That's what I am saying to you," said Ari. "That is why you need me."

"Ari, the Marshals. The Marshals are so onto you. They won't stand by and let you shine them on. What are you using to think with? Is your brain fried from drugs?"

"You don't understand," said Ari.

"You're so smart. You promised them the moon and stars. You promised them me. But they don't need you anymore. Everything you promised them I've already given them, including the rest of Raleigh's ledgers."

"Connie," said Ari. "No, you didn't."

"They don't need you to run East-West for them because then they would have to trust you, which, with good reason, they don't. So now that you're of no further use, the next step is they find a dark hole for you under a jail somewhere. And that dream you had about a new life and a new identity in a beautiful place like this one, maybe, after it's all over, is never going to happen, Ari. They've got you for pimping, if nothing else, here at The Lodge, and maybe murder. They're not going to let that ride. The task force has no more need of your services. I can call Marshal Ventine for you. You can tell him not to say, dream on."

"Why do you hurt me so?" said Ari.

"What hurts, Ari? I know it's not your heart."

"What hurts, Con? What hurts?" Ari looked off over the ocean. "What hurts the most is knowing you are right."

Constance noted the chill in his tone. She took another step back and said, "Goodbye, Ari."

"Don't go yet, Con. Stay a while, please." He reached out while she was backing up. She turned away from him to head back up the ramp.

"Connie, please," he called out to her, "come back. I'll let you blow me."

She kept on and hurried up the steps and past the fountain. She crossed the courtyard and took the stairs down to the parking garage. She stepped clear of the stairwell and encountered Bob, walking past on his way back to the shop.

Unexpectedly, she caught up to him and took his arm.

"Bob," she said, "where is Mr. Ventine?"

"I don't know," said Bob. "He could be anywhere."

"Bob, stay with me awhile, please. I'm very frightened of Ari."

"Alright," said Bob. The maintenance shop was a hundred feet away. Inside was safety.

Ed Nogg had picked that day to have a colonoscopy, so he was not about and not expected to appear. In his absence, Bob was in charge.

CHAPTER TWENTY-NINE
DARK HEART

The immigrant boy, all grown up, Aronoyad Wilgushku sat alone on the top step at the far end of the north beach ramp. He watched a pod of porpoises at play heading north as a long line of pelicans swooped over them heading south, each bird in turn wetting breast feathers on a rippling swell. The blue-gray ocean glinted in the glare of the noon sun. He took off his sunglasses and wiped his eyes. No one would have believed that he could still weep for a past that never was. Their son would have been twenty-six, had he lived. Their whole lives would have been different.

The mistakes he had made as a young man were not the same mistakes he would have made as a young father. If Constance had not fallen out of love with him, where would he be now? Who would he be?

She had said that he was never a child, but she was wrong. He had loved with an innocent heart once.

He watched the pod of playful dolphins moving through the waves, never losing their true north.

Ari looked behind him and saw David Moriarty standing by the railing at the fountain courtyard. Ari stood up and waved, and David came down the steps and walked out to meet him.

Ari smiled, "Hello, David. I am sorry things did not work out so well for you."

"Things did not work out well, no," said David.

"How can I help you, David?"

"Ari. Mr. Wilkes," said David, "the best thing you can do for me is pack up your little band of gypsies, pay your bills and get the hell out of my hotel."

"David, have I offended you in some way?"

"Offended me? You ruined me. You put that coke in my pocket."

"I, sir? No, not I," said Ari.

"You saw my weakness. That's how you do it. You find weaknesses and exploit them."

"I fear my welcome here grows thin," said Ari.

"Who are you?" David asked. "Why did you come here? There's nothing for you here. What do you want?"

"I wanted your job," said Ari. "I don't anymore. Now I just want to kill somebody, maybe a few people."

Ari pulled a pistol from his coat pocket. "You'll do," he said. "For a start."

"Dude," said David, "put that thing away."

Ari attached a silencer to the pistol, raised it and shot David in the center of his forehead. The back of David's head sprayed out over the dune, and his body blew back over the railing into the sand.

"Mr. Entitlement," said Ari. He pocketed the gun.

He looked up at the Lodge and saw no one on any of the balconies. He gave a little wave to anyone who might be watching a monitor and headed back up the ramp. It was always going to end like this. He had known it all his life.

He punched a button on his phone to ring Mikhail.

"Where is Connie?"

"In the maintenance shop with Bob."

•　　•　　•　　•　　•

In the back of the paint section of the shop, Karl was engaged in his own 'green' project, the recycling of dirty mineral spirits. He had two tightly lidded heavy duty plastic two-gallon buckets filled with used paint thinner. Left to settle over time, the paint solids from many colors of alkyd paints and stains congealed, forming mud-colored oleaginous pancakes on the bottoms of the buckets while the liquid clarified to a yellowish transparency. Karl poured off the clean dirty spirits into a fresh bucket and scraped the paint gunk into the trash.

Paint thinner was expensive, and recycling made sense, but it required a certain commitment. The smell was like no other, cloying, sickly-sweet and faintly putrid.

Karl had a procedure that he modified, periodically. When he had oil brushes to wash, voila, using the recycled spirits for the first and second rinses allowed him to reserve new thinner for final rinses.

A giant exhaust fan mounted into the wall sucked the odor out of the shop quickly, but it was very loud.

With the roaring hum of the exhaust fan dominating the shop, Bob and Constance entered without seeing Karl. Bob knew that Karl was back in his paint section, but he didn't mention it to Constance.

"Can we turn that fan off?" Constance yelled.

"What?"

Constance was yelling again, "Can we turn that fan off?" when Karl cut the fan off.

"It's off," said Bob, in the sudden silence.

"Hey," Karl called out, still absorbed in his alchemy, "I'll cut it back on in a minute." He turned on an inside fan set at medium speed to circulate air and allow private conversations on the other end of the shop. There were two big wall unit air conditioners, as well, one on each end that kept the shop chilled in the heat of summer. But only the big suction fan could vacuum out the smell.

"Hi Karl," Constance called into the abyss of the paint shop.

Bob walked out to his truck and removed his gun kit from the glove box. When he brought it back into the shop, Constance asked, "What's that?"

Bob ejected a clip, reloaded, pulled the slide and set the safety. He kept a "Code Brown" bag by the door, a long zippered cloth bag with plungers and toilet tools at the ready. He put his gun in the bag, zipped it closed and set it back behind the door.

"Bob, what are you doing?" Constance asked.

"I'm trying not to react to your tone," he said, "since, obviously, you can't help it."

"Help what?" she shrilled. "What are you talking about?"

"Nothing," said Bob. "Never mind."

Ari and Mikhail were coming. They were walking down the center of the parking garage toward the shop, close enough for Ari to call out in mockery, "Hello, Maintenance."

"Don't let him in," said Constance. "Do not let him in."

Ari and Mikhail could be seen through the gap that existed between the two solid doors when they were closed. They could also see Bob and Constance peering back at them through the gap, as well. It was that wide. The exhaust fan kicked on again with a roar that was much louder inside the shop. Bob opened the door, stepped out of the shop and closed it behind him. He carried his Code Brown bag.

The fan noise stopped.

"That's one big fan," said Ari.

"It is indeed," said Bob.

"I come in peace," Ari said.

"That remains to be seen," said Bob.

"Bob, do you have any duct tape?" Mikhail asked.

"We need duct tape," said Ari.

"I hesitate to ask what for," said Bob.

"So she won't get away. Ha!" Ari laughed. "You ever hear that joke?"

"No," said Bob, "how's it go?"

Ari smiled. "Let's go inside and talk."

Bob said, "This area is restricted to Lodge personnel. I don't admit hotel guests in the shop anymore."

Ari nodded. "Experience is the best teacher. It is proven fact."

"We still need duct tape," said Mikhail.

Bob looked curiously at Mikhail, "Weren't you fired a little while ago?"

Mikhail's eyes fell. "Yes," he said.

"No duct tape for you," said Bob.

Ari smiled again. "You put up noble resistance, Bob Day. I admire your gumption. Now, I wish to speak with my beloved."

Bob lifted his code brown bag, unzipped it and drew his pistol in one continuous motion. Mikhail also had a pistol in hand, pointed up.

"I'm pretty sure she doesn't want to talk to anybody," said Bob.

"Connie, honey, please, babycakes," Ari wheedled through the door in a parody of wheedling, "let my love open the door to your heart."

"Ari, go away," Constance called out to him through the door.

Ari leaned one cheek against the door and crooned into the crack, with one eye on Bob and half a smile directed at him. "Connie, Connie, Connie. Must I sodomize you yet again?"

"Ari, you are insane."

"Or kill you? Choose. Sodomy or death?"

Bob said, "Enough." He pointed his gun at Ari.

Mikhail pointed his gun at Bob.

Ari laughed at the threat of gunplay.

"Don't shoot, Bob. And by that, I mean also Mikhail, don't shoot Bob. Interesting, is it not, how the threat of sodomy invariably provokes a response? What a puzzler for the human genome project, yes? Bob, do you believe in reincarnation?"

"Not a lot," said Bob.

"I have lived this life many times," said Ari. "I have been here before, and so have you. You guarded the gates of Trinosophia in the time of St. Germain."

"Did I?"

"Yes, and I killed you," said Ari. "But first I profaned your holy of holies in the name of Baphomet."

"So now you're back," said Bob.

"Bob, have you ever had a grudge fuck? Maybe with your ex-wife, some woman you loved who ground your nuts to powder? Then, one day you fucked her so hard you could almost believe she would stay fucked and content herself for the rest of her life with the memory of that one stern fucking. Have you ever had a grudge fuck like that, Bob?"

"I would have remembered," said Bob.

"It was like that for me with Connie. I'm going to grudge fuck her one last time. Then you can kill me. Are you prepared to kill me?"

"I'll stop you," said Bob.

"You must kill me to stop me," said Ari. He put his lips to the crack between the doors and whispered, "Connie, your negative energy is emanating into the atmosphere. Later, we'll go dancing. And celebrate."

"I have nothing to say to you," said Constance.

"I have so much to say to you, and so little time. The authorities will be here soon and then perhaps we all will die. Open the door or I shoot Saint Bob. I assure you, even though he has a gun pointed at my brain right now, he will not risk his sainthood. I can do as I like. He is a hesitator."

"Just stay inside," said Bob.

"Cousin," said Mikhail, "This is not the way to Canada."

Ari sighed, "Go. Go to Canada. Wait, give me the gun."

Mikhail stepped back and leveled the gun at Ari. "No."

Ari calmly drew his own gun out and shot Mikhail in the heart as Mikhail fired blanks at Ari. "Idiot," said Ari. "You are not my cousin."

Bob stood by with his own gun in his hand. He had made no attempt to fire it. He felt paralyzed by inaction, yet he kept his gun trained on Ari.

Constance stood back from the door she had quietly unlocked before she heard the gunshot. She was armed with a hammer in one hand and a propane torch in the other.

"It's open," she said.

Ari pushed the door open wide. "Come on, Saint Bob," he said. "Let's go to hell."

CHAPTER THIRTY
DIRTY SPIRITS

Bob followed Ari into the shop, a step and a half behind.

The truth, that he was so easily read that Ari could turn his back on him and know with perfect confidence that Bob would neither shoot to kill nor even fire his weapon, paralyzed Bob's mind like a koan too profound to fathom.

Ari swatted aside the unlit torch Constance tried to wield against him and caught her other wrist as she swung a claw hammer at his head. In one series of moves he disarmed her, twisted her left arm behind her back, held the pistol to her head, and pushed her face down on the workbench.

Bob pointed his gun at Ari's head. "Let her go," he said.

"Shoot, Bob," said Ari. He pressed himself against her hips and grunted. He let go of her wrist long enough to unzip his pants. Freed of its confines, his priapic anomaly unfurled itself and reared its ugly head.

Karl approached from his end of the shop with two white Styrofoam coffee cups in his hands filled with paint gunk from the bottom of a dirty spirits bucket. He'd been in the back filling cups with paint gunk, each with a two-minute shelf life.

Styrofoam was not a valid container for solvent waste. In two minutes or less, the gunk would melt the Styrofoam.

The first cup Karl threw hit the left side of Ari's face.

Purplish alkyd paint solids smeared across his cheek and one side of his nose. He leered at Karl like a wild Pict warrior. "You're next, painter," he warned as Constance twisted against him. He tugged at her waistband. Buttons popped.

With the gun at her head, he caught her wrist again and held her pinned.

Mauve paint jelly dripped down the front of his shirt. A globule dropped on her lower back, oozed down and pooled in the valley above the crack of her ass.

"What is that shit? It burns," she screamed.

The second cup hit Ari between the eyes. He let go of Constance to wipe his eyes. The sludge stung the tender flesh around the rims of his eyelids and began to burn. He held them closed and wiped his face with his sleeve while Constance veered off to a second workbench. She scooped up an awl and flung it at him. At the same moment, Bob overcame his hesitancy and ventured a shot at the gun in Ari's hand. He couldn't bring himself to shoot a kill shot point blank or even to shoot at his gun hand. The bullet ricocheted off the handle of the iron vise attached to the work table. A sliver of chrome sent airborne by the ricochet nicked a bloody gash in Ari's earlobe.

Ari's mouth opened to groan, and the steel heel of the awl collided with his teeth and upper lip and chipped a tooth. He spat blood on the worktable, picked up the awl. Blood stained the front of his shirt. He held the awl in one hand and the gun in the other. He waved them back and forth like a blind man pointing and lunging at shadows. His eyes were burning.

He croaked, "Kill me, bitches! You can't!"

Karl pressed the thumb switch igniter on the blow torch and directed the four-inch flame at Ari's gun hand. Ari dropped the gun on the table when his hand caught fire. The paint gunk ignited, and his shirt and face and hair burst into flames.

Fire covered him. Ari screamed. His agony shocked Bob into action.

Bob put his gun down, took the fire extinguisher from its hook and sprayed fire retardant all over Ari, staunching the flames before they spread. Ari was still alive, covered with fire retardant and third-degree burns. He writhed on the concrete floor, a specter of hellish torment. Both hands gripped his charred penis, still pink-tipped and throbbing like a dog's insistent tail.

"God damn Viagra," he said. "God damn these four-hour erections."

"Try not to think about the pain," said Constance. "Focus on the happy times."

"Please," Ari begged her. His blackened fingers scrabbled like a crab claw for the awl on the floor where it had rolled beyond his reach.

Bob hung up the office phone. "EMTs on the way," he said.

"Give it to me," Ari commanded.

Constance picked the awl up from the floor. "This thingy? Why should I?"

"You owe me!" Ari bellowed.

"Suffer," said Constance.

Karl held his palm out to her. She put the awl in Karl's hand. He squatted down in front of Ari and put it in Ari's hand.

Karl stepped back.

Ari's burning eyes found Bob. He said, "Saint Bob. Leave dirty work to sinners."

Ari placed the point of the awl in the hollow above his eyeball and drove the spike to the hilt into his brain with the heel of his own hand in a single thrust.

He collapsed and quivered for some time after. Death came slowly.

"Who was that guy?" said Karl.

CHAPTER THIRTY-ONE
NAM MAIOR LAUS TABERNUS

Detective Billy Carlisle took the call out to the Lodge. He'd been idling in the area, monitoring on the radio the departure of the Marshals Service from the surveillance business. With local liaisons terminated, the Joint Task Force had disbanded as soon as the FBI pulled out. The Marshals were gone from their construction trailer.

Something was going on at the Lodge.

Detective Carlisle arrived soon after the Fire Chief and the EMTs. He pulled up in front of the building on the north end near the parking garage exit area nearest the maintenance shop.

An old acquaintance of his father's, Karl Legume, the painter, leaned back against the stucco wall in a patch of sunshine.

"Hey, Billy," said Karl, at the detective's approach.

"Karl, what are we looking at?"

"You'll have to see it to believe it," said Karl.

The detective followed Karl in through the exit. Mikhail's body lay where he had fallen.

"Who shot him?" he asked.

"Dick Head," said Karl.

"Who?" Detective Carlisle asked.

"I used to call him the Sultan. I changed it to Dolomite because he was obsessed with his prodigious member, but nobody got that reference, not even Bob. I thought Dolomite was famous. Come to find out nobody remembers Dolomite. So that guy's nickname is Dick Head. That's plain enough."

"What's his real name, Karl?" Detective Carlisle asked.

"How the fuck would I know that?" said Karl.

Detective Carlisle said, "Don't go anywhere, Karl. I'll need to take your statement."

The Fire Chief stepped out of the maintenance shop and met the detective outside the double doors.

"Bill, the paint shop's loaded with flammables. They need a fire safety warning and a commendation for not burning this place down."

Inside the shop, the Chief kept talking. "You ever hear of suicide by spontaneous combustion? Me either."

. . . . .

Detective Carlisle came out of the shop and found Karl again in the same place, leaning against the stucco wall in the same patch of sunlight.

"Come on, Karl," he said. "Suicide?"

"Do you have a tape recorder?" Karl asked.

"I have a digital."

"Take my statement so I can go home."

Detective Carlisle produced a small recorder, switched it on and said, by way of introduction, "This is eyewitness Karl Legume's statement. Suppose you start at the beginning, Karl, and tell us in your own words what happened here."

"Well, first of all, Sparky in there was about to ream Constance out right in front of us unless somebody stopped him. Bob could have shot him, but he didn't because that's exactly what Dolomite wanted him to do.

"I threw paint scum in his eyes. But he never let go of the gun."

"Dolomite had a gun?" said Detective Carlisle.

"Don't call him Dolomite," said Karl. "It's insulting when you do it. Have some respect. His name was Wilkes, and he held a gun to her head. Bob had his gun aimed at him. I lit the blowtorch and burned Wilkes' gun hand. That made him drop the gun. Then he spontaneously combusted.

"He must have had spilled liquor on his shirt sleeve to go off like he did. Paint scum is not that flammable. He flared up like a marshmallow. Then he took the awl and drove it right into his eyeball. I saw him do it. I'll swear to it. Nobody touched him till the EMTs came."

"Karl," said Detective Carlisle, "did you know that man at all?"

"He was a guest. That's all I knew."

Detective Carlisle clicked the recorder off.

"How'd he get a hold of the awl if he was blinded by, what? Paint scum?"

"I don't know," said Karl. "He had it in his hand."

"He dropped the gun when his hand caught on fire but held on to the awl the whole time he was burning?"

"Maybe it fused to his hand in the fire," said Karl.

"The wood handle's not blackened," said Detective Carlisle.

"Then I don't fucking know," said Karl.

"Was Wilkes standing upright when Bob sprayed him with fire retardant?"

"He had already fallen," said Karl.

"If he had the awl in hand until he fell and dropped it, how far could it have rolled?"

"Not far," said Karl.

"Must have been within reach," said Detective Carlisle, "maybe just inches away from his hand. If he wasn't completely blinded, he probably could have seen it."

"If you were a Viking," said Karl, "you'd understand what it means to die with a sword in your hand."

"Karl. Listen to me, Karl," said Detective Carlisle. "That man was not a Viking. You're in a state of shock. You need to take a few hours and settle down. People in shock may not realize they're in shock. They go on talking without thinking and can get themselves in trouble by talking too much to the wrong people. I terminated this interview for your own good, Karl. And I suggest you don't give any more interviews today."

"You think there's a more genteel way to tell this story?" said Karl.

"I hope there is," said Detective Carlisle, "because that story is unfit for popular consumption." He looked around and spoke in a low tone, "You just confessed to a police officer to setting a man on fire. Your best bet is not to talk to anybody for awhile."

"Billy," said Karl, "You have real good forensics people back at the lab where his body's headed, don't you? You better have CSI Belle Rive on hand, because they're going to have to identify fifty-eight different kinds of paint and determine batch numbers and which paint store each paint came from. I mean, if they're going to be thorough, in order to know the exact solvent base of the alleged accelerant. Until they know that, they don't know shit. That paint gunk is more paint solids than solvents. You ever try to light a can of paint on fire? Good luck. I rest my case. You'd have to prove that paint gunk made him flame on. All I lit was his hand on the gun, and that was self-defense. What of it? Are your forensics people that good? I fucking doubt it. Let them figure out what happened. Have at it. I'm just telling you so you'll know the truth. He rammed that awl into his own eye. That was a Viking suicide."

"Okay, Karl. Thanks," said Detective Carlisle.

"I probably ought to take your advice," said Karl. "Go the fuck home and shut up."

"That's what I'd do," said Detective Carlisle.

"I can't wind down," said Karl. "I need to talk it out. Turn that tape back on, motherfucker, I'm not done yet."

"Karl, I'm a cop, son," said Detective Carlisle. "Do you know what that means?"

"Son? I whipped your daddy's ass," said Karl.

"The hell you did. Look here, Karl, before you get belligerent with anybody else, take a look around at where you are. See that yellow tape? That's not wet paint tape. That's crime scene tape."

"Now that's just uncalled for," said Karl.

"You've got a long night ahead of you if you plan to stick around for press interviews. You better keep your head. Now where's Bob?"

"Over there," said Karl, indicating the EMT vehicle.

Constance was on a gurney being loaded into an ambulance. One of the EMTs invited Bob to come along. He declined, and they closed the back doors.

The ambulance pulled away from the curb. Bob walked over to join Karl and Bill.

"Bill," he said, nodding.

"Hello, Bob," said Detective Carlisle. "Good to see you in one piece."

Bob turned to Karl. "Pope, how you doing?"

"I'm jacked up skyward, Bob," said Karl. "I can't shut up. I need a drink. Bob, you and me, we need to have a drink."

"Or three or four," said Bob. "Unfortunately, there's been a new development. They found David Moriarty shot dead on the beach by the north ramp."

"Oh, hell," said Detective Carlisle. "I'm going to have to ask both of you to stick around awhile longer."

"When it rains, it pours," said Bob.

· · · · ·

"When did you two get palsy?" Karl asked, after the detective walked off to catch up with events.

"Recently," said Bob.

"What's the story?" said Karl. "Are you a ninja, Bob? Is that it? Are you my ninja?"

"You're the ninja," said Bob.

"Pope. Is that my nickname?"

"You didn't know?" said Bob.

"I always wondered if you had a nickname for me other than the mad painter."

"Well, you wear white and sometimes you pontificate," said Bob.

"It never took though, did it," said Karl.

"We didn't want you to get a big head," said Bob.

"We? You got a mouse in your pocket?"

Bob smiled. "Karl, up until today, I've been in the witness protection program."

"Me too," said Karl.

"Really?" said Bob.

"No, not really," said Karl. "What?"

"I had to keep it secret," said Bob.

"I can see why," said Karl. "This is your past catching up to you."

"A subject for another day," said Bob. "Right now, you need to take my advice. Don't talk anymore. Don't volunteer any information to anyone for any reason. Get through today and don't talk. You don't have to. When the media gets here, they'll act like they own your story. They don't."

"Bob, I have a loose tongue," said Karl. "I'm not the ninja. I'm not even a ninja. Here you are, leading an undercover life. You brought grace to the most tedious days of my life. You made it possible for me to stand working here for five years. I've dreaded this day, and now it's come. You'll be moving on, and I'll be stuck here with no one to talk to and what an ass boring tragedy that will be for me."

172

"I know somebody who might be able to help," said Bob.

"Billy asked how Sparky got the awl. I told him I didn't know. I don't know why I held that back. He turned the tape off on me. I was just getting warmed up. I hadn't even got to that part yet. He's trying to rush me. Get to the point, all that, trying to trip me up, confuse me. Fuck him. I didn't murder that fucker. I just set him on fire. Thanks for putting it out, by the way. Damn, you were fast, Bob. You were so fucking efficient. I didn't even know we had fire extinguishers."

"Yes, you did," said Bob.

"I need to keep this job, if I can," said Karl. "Much as I hate to admit it, I need this monkey job. I can't be without a job at my age."

"Well, you may lose this one," said Bob.

"I know. They won't keep me on after this. I can't get along with Ed anyway, not without you in the buffer zone. What else can I do? Paint houses. Drive a cab. I should host a talk radio show. Interview people, tell them how fucked up they are. Any idea how to get there from here, Bob? I've been more or less a failure in life, as far as goals achieved and financial success, but this thing today feels like there ought to be a payday in it somewhere."

"You're not going to shut up, are you?" said Bob.

"I can't, Bob. For the Greater Glory of the Lodge."

Over Karl's shoulder, Bob saw Berne Ventine emerge from a black sedan. Berne made brief eye contact with Bob and let his roaming gaze settle on Detective Carlisle. Berne approached him with a grave demeanor.

"Detective Carlisle," said Berne. "Sorry I'm late. We had urgent business down near Tampa this morning. Gibsontown, where all the old carnies go to die. What a day. I was two hours out when Mikhail called."

Detective Carlisle said, "Well, it seems like it all just went bad for nothing. Unless your urgent business in Gibsontown paid off."

"I wouldn't say for nothing," said Berne. "I can't account the cost at this time."

"Well, Marshal," said Detective Carlisle. "It's your show."

"No sir," said Berne. "All I want is my guys the fuck out of here. This is your puppy."

"Which guys would those be?" asked Detective Carlisle.

"These two corpses. And Bob, if he'll have me. You can have Moriarty."

"I can't believe Wilkes was your guy, too," said Detective Carlisle.

"Our embarrassment," said Berne. "Your point?"

"David Moriarty is a huge loss for this community. You can't sweep his death under the rug," said Detective Carlisle.

"I wouldn't do that," said Berne. "The press needs a story. What happened here? Let's ask our first responder, Detective Carlisle."

Berne gestured as if a microphone was in his hand. He blew on it and test tapped it with a finger and thrust it forward rudely in Detective Carlisle's face.

"Detective, what happened here?"

Detective Carlisle raised a hand to ward off the imaginary microphone. "Belle Rive County is shocked and saddened today by the murders of David Moriarty, General Manager of the Belle Rive Lodge and Club and Mikhail Bulbek, a bellman, and also by the suicide of the gunman who took hostages in the maintenance shop and set himself on fire."

"Can you pretty that up?" Berne asked.

"What do you suggest?" Detective Carlisle asked.

"Lee J. Wilkes shot and killed David Moriarty and Mikhail Bulbek before committing suicide. Funeral arrangements are being handled privately. End of statement. Let them choke on it. Etcetera. Update to follow."

"You make it sound mundane," said Detective Carlisle.

"It's a lot to fall into, Bill," said Berne. "A deep and wide sea of mundanity. Most people never see the shore."

"There's no way I can stonewall the press on this," said Detective Carlisle.

"I can," said Berne.

Detective Carlisle shrugged. "Okay, Marshal. Show me how it's done."

•　　　•　　　•

The bodies of Mikhail Bulbek, Lee J. Wilkes and David Moriarty were loaded away in ambulances in transit to destinations unknown. The media was unaccountably delayed.

"I invoked a jurisdictional imperative on their ass," said Berne Ventine, expansive in triumph. "A statutory abuse of power but there you have it. Shit will not grow in a vacuum."

He addressed Bob and Karl. Detective Carlisle stood beside him.

Berne smiled. "I want you guys out of here. Karl, good to meet you. Go home. Do nothing. Bob, how's breakfast in Bunkie sound right about now?"

"Better," said Bob, "but look, Berne, Karl's in shock."

"I'm not in shock," said Karl, "I'm just going to miss you, Bob, that's all."

"Well, what have we here?" said Detective Carlisle.

"I'm going to miss my friend," said Karl. "Get your mind out of the gutter, dickhead. Wipe that smirk off your face."

"I'm not so sure I'll have to go anywhere," said Bob. "Now that it's over."

"If you stick around, the story comes out," said Berne. "Leave, and the story leaves with you. Karl, you'll be here. The story is yours as long as you don't tell it. As soon as you do, it's not yours anymore."

"My story?" said Karl, "I don't even know it."

"You're better off," said Berne. "Trust me." He shook Karl's hand. "Don't worry about a thing. You're golden."

"Berne," said Bob, "I can't go to Bunkie."

"Well, then, Bob," said Berne, "I'll give you a few minutes to reconsider."

"Detective," he nodded to Bill Carlisle, "a word?"

Berne stepped off with Detective Carlisle for a confidential moment. They walked toward the black sedan. Berne inclined his head toward Bill's ear. "I'm told there are some telling comments handwritten by Mr. Wilkes on comment cards."

"Comment cards," said Detective Carlisle.

"Worth looking into," said Berne. "See you back at the ranch."

Berne stepped into the black sedan and disappeared down the boulevard, his exit timed to the minute before the network news van arrived.

Bob and Karl rode the golf cart down to Housekeeping to punch out. On their return, newsman Christopher Faircloth was interviewing Marvin Gardener. Karl parked the cart and headed for his car. Bob hung back.

"I better wait around awhile," said Bob. "I need to call Ed."

"You already punched out," said Karl.

"I have some loose ends to tie up," said Bob.

"I guess we're not going to have that drink," said Karl.

"Not today," said Bob.

"Alright, Bob," said Karl. "Adios, muchacho."

Bob watched Karl's old Volvo exit the parking garage past the media truck. He wished they could have had that drink.

• • • • • •

Berne returned to face the media with a second Marshal who quietly seated Bob in the back of the sedan. He took Bob's keys and drove Bob's truck out of the parking garage past the media tableau by the boulevard where Berne Ventine was addressing the television audience while newsman Christopher Faircloth looked on, holding a microphone.

"Today, two tragic murders illustrate the need for constant vigilance. Our future as a society depends on our dedication to our mission to protect and serve communities. Our hearts and our support are with the victims' families and loved ones as we promise and assure them that their lives will be remembered. To ensure that these are not empty words, the U. S. Marshals Service is endowing the newly formed David O. Moriarty Foundation with grant funding and a mandate to build in Belle Rive County a much needed state-of-the-art laboratory facility for the study of forensic medicine."

The driver and Bob watched Berne wrap it up by pretending to silence his humming cell phone.

"Right about now," said the driver.

"Nam Maior Laus Tabernus," said Bob, to no one.

On the live feed television in the sedan, Bob watched newsman Christopher Faircloth ask Berne Ventine the question, "What happened here today?"

Berne held up one finger as he put his phone to his ear.

"Okay," he said, slapping it closed.

"We'll have to wait for the answers to that question," said Berne. He smiled for the camera and said, "Excuse me, I have to go now."

A technician unclipped the microphone from his collar and Berne climbed into the back of the black sedan beside Bob.

"I have mixed feelings about this," said Bob.

"Bob, I will watch over him like a shepherd," Berne promised. "I give you my word."

"And Ed, you'll talk to Ed?"

"I will talk to Ed," said Berne. "Go," he told the driver.

"I can't go home?" said Bob.

"No, you can't go home. This car takes you to the airport."

"Not to Bunkie."

"No, not to Bunkie," said Berne.

"Where?"

"You'll see when you get there," said Berne.

Bob leaned back against the leather seats. He closed his eyes, not liking not leaving behind any kind of note to let the few individuals who would miss him know that he would miss them, too. No such note or memo could be left behind. His was an erasable existence.

If he stayed, he would have to answer questions. His fellow employees would learn soon enough that for four years he had walked among them, as one of them, without anyone ever knowing much about him. That was over. He had to go. It was time, and it didn't matter where.

CHAPTER THIRTY-TWO
ANOTHER DAY IN PARADISE

Claudia was running down the beach. Prancing.

"See how she prances," Bob would say, transfixed as he was by her.

Every Claudia sighting was an event. One could experience a feeling of rejuvenation just by watching her pass.

Karl watched Claudia run to the north from the oceanfront balcony of one of the rooms. He was touching up rust stains on the patio and feeling sorry for himself for continuing to live so pathetically mired in tedium day after day like a little monkey on a leash.

Claudia was so beautiful. And Bob was so gone.

Everyone in the hotel business was supposed to be replaceable. That was one of the tenets of the faith. And it was true. Even Bob. Even David Moriarty.

Ed Nogg took the helm of the Lodge as acting General Manager. Karl was offered the opportunity to enroll in management training. If he chose to step up and embrace the training, he could possibly qualify to be considered for the Head of Maintenance position that would open up if Ed Nogg worked out as General Manager.

Constance had quit the Lodge. Upon release from the hospital, she contacted Duncan Upton and sold him her five shares. She was gone, back to Wimauma.

Curiosity ebbed in the days following the murders. Why was so little written about them in the paper and so little commentary on the television news? Some blamed a federal anti-embarrassment clause in a statute regarding national security. Others said that was nonsense.

Nobody knew anything, and nobody needed to know anything.

Nobody asked the right questions.

Everything at the Lodge kept on going much as it had before. Renaldo, reinstated, still sang a capella in the kitchen and greeted guests with a friendly attitude and loved to remind us all that every day was "Another Day in Paradise."

It did not seem like just another day to Karl, nor did it seem like Paradise, except while watching Claudia run. She turned and ran south again, back toward the Lodge. Karl watched her from a distance as she passed by, running so gracefully down the hard sand near the water.

• • • • •

Shania kept working on an update to her timeline. She couldn't say for whose edification it was meant. If only for her own, then it was failing. There were too many blank areas, too many gaps. There was no one else her timeline edified, and no one other than Billy Carlisle who cared about the timeline of the story she had broken and nurtured and followed and updated only to have her editor tell her to leave it alone. She didn't like leaving it alone.

Detective Carlisle had released a number of statements to the press. He had refused all requests for interviews, even Shania Doyle's.

Unofficially, he would talk to her, but he was no longer a fountain of secrets.

Shania had visited Constance Featherton in the hospital and had heard her tale of attempted rape. Her paper was not interested in that story at all. They wanted the David Moriarty story.

Constance claimed for herself the pivotal role in her former lover's psychological collapse. She claimed to have crushed his ego thoroughly prior to the murder of David Moriarty. His assault on her in the maintenance shop was a death wish enacted after she had derailed his dreams and left him with no reason to live.

Karl Legume had refused several times to talk to Shania Doyle. Shania kept dropping by the maintenance shop to see if he would reconsider. One day, she brought her timeline with her, and he agreed to take a look at it.

Shania learned that Karl's perspective was rooted in the daily details of life at the Lodge and focused on the single moment of confrontation in the maintenance shop, where good and evil had clashed over epic, ancient codes and the tarnished honor of the captive maiden was restored.

He knew nothing other than hearsay about the deaths of Senator Rutland and Raleigh Featherton. He knew none of the Alabama history that preceded Bob's relocation to the Lodge.

Unconcerned with all that other background, Karl's one area of direct knowledge corresponded with the biggest blank spots in Shania's timeline.

"I can see that we might have something to offer each other," said Karl.

"What can you offer me?" Shania asked.

"Besides an ending for your book?" said Karl.

"Who says I'm writing a book?"

"You would if you knew how to end it," said Karl.

"What do you want from me?" she asked.

"I don't want to run the maintenance department, I'll tell you that."

"I can't offer you a job," she said.

"What do I get in return for my story?"

"I can't promise you anything," she said.

"Will I be famous?"

"No."

"Will I be rich?"

"Not likely."

"Que sera, sera," said Karl. "You have a tape recorder?"

NOTE FROM THE AUTHOR

Word-of-mouth is crucial for any author to succeed. If you enjoyed the book, please leave a review online—anywhere you are able. Even if it's just a sentence or two. It would make all the difference and would be very much appreciated.

Thanks!
K. C. Wilson

ABOUT THE AUTHOR

K. C. Wilson, a North Florida writer, is the author of *The Route*, songwriter for *The Rubes*, a 2012 Nilsen Prize finalist and winner of the 2016 Wexford Film Festival Screenplay contest. His short fiction, nonfiction and poetry appears in various publications such as *Opossum*, *New Southern Fugitives*, *Cavalier*, *Think Journal*, *Faraway Journal*, *Sheepshead Review* and *Kerouac's Dog*. *Saint Bob Day* is his second novel.

Thank you so much for reading one of our **Dark Humor** novels.

If you enjoyed our book, please check out our recommended title for your next great read!

Managed Care by Joe Barrett

"Witty, occasionally crass, and an unqualified delight." –*KIRKUS REVIEWS*

View other Black Rose Writing titles at
www.blackrosewriting.com/books and use promo code
PRINT to receive a **20% discount** when purchasing.